"This doesn't need to be difficult, just let me tell him you are...*you*. Okay?"

Toben stared at her, her words making no sense. "You lost me."

She glared at him, pure hostility rolling off her tiny frame. "Rowdy knows Toben Boone is his father. But you didn't introduce yourself, so he doesn't know *you* are Toben Boone. I'd rather have that conversation with him, alone. Like we've been for the last seven years."

Toben felt numb all over. "Rowdy?" He swallowed, unable to breathe, to think, to process what the hell she was saying.

"That was Rowdy," she repeated, her irritation mounting. She looked ready to rip into him.

"I don't know what you're talking about, Poppy. But if you're trying to tell me I'm a father..." He sucked in a deep breath, his chest hurting so bad he pressed a hand over his heart. "Don't you think you waited a little long to tell me I have a son?"

Dear Reader,

Welcome back to Stonewall Crossing! The Boones (and I) are happy you stopped by! The brothers might be happily married, but there are plenty of Boones in need of a match.

Toben Boone spent his life avoiding love and commitment, and he didn't think he was missing a thing. Of course, that's when love normally comes knocking. Love, in Toben's case, comes wrapped up in the feisty form of Poppy White. The one woman who made him feel something deep down in his heart.

Poppy White was ready to start her new life off the rodeo circuit. She and her son, Rowdy, can't wait to make their little farm and Stonewall Crossing home. But running into the sweet-talking, lady-chasing, heart-breaking cowboy that left her high and dry when she needed help most is anything but a pleasant surprise. Having Toben Boone around stirs up all sorts of feelings, some good, some not so good, and she's not sure what to do about it.

I adore this story—all the passion and hurt and fun and healing warmed my heart. I hope their love story speaks to you, too. Be on the lookout for Tandy's book this winter. Nothing like a dreamy cowboy to warm things up on a cold night. I love to hear from readers, so drop me an email anytime at sasha@sashasummers.com.

Thanks so much for reading!

Sasha

A SON FOR
THE COWBOY

———

SASHA SUMMERS

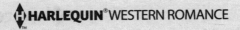

Recycling programs for this product may not exist in your area.

ISBN-13: 978-0-373-75766-4

A Son for the Cowboy

Copyright © 2017 by Sasha Best

This edition published by arrangement with Harlequin Books S.A.

For questions and comments about the quality of this book, please contact us at CustomerService@Harlequin.com.

Printed in U.S.A.

Sasha Summers grew up surrounded by books. Her passions have always been storytelling, romance and travel. Whether it's an easy-on-the-eyes cowboy or a hero of truly mythic proportions, Sasha falls a little in love with each and every one of her heroes. She frequently gets lost with her characters in the worlds she creates, forgetting those everyday tasks like laundry and dishes. Luckily, her four brilliant children and hero-inspiring hubby are super understanding and helpful.

Books by Sasha Summers

Harlequin Western Romance

The Boones of Texas

A Cowboy's Christmas Reunion
Twins for the Rebel Cowboy
Courted by the Cowboy
A Cowboy to Call Daddy

Harlequin Blaze

Seducing the Best Man
Christmas in His Bed

Visit the Author Profile page
at Harlequin.com for more titles.

This is for all the couples that had to fall apart to fall back together again. Love is never easy.

Thank you to my brainstorming partners, Joni Hahn, Marnie Culver and Frances Kiana, and to my amazing, fantastic readers!

Chapter One

Poppy tucked a brown curl behind her ear and rested her chin on her steering wheel, admiring the denim-clad rear of the big, brawny cowboy peering in the picture window of her newly purchased storefront. Those jeans should be downright illegal. Or the rear that was wearing them should. Something about a nice butt in a work-worn pair of Wranglers got her every time. Hey, she appreciated beauty where she saw it.

"This it, Ma?" Rowdy asked, his sleep-thickened voice ending her ogling.

"This is it," she said, smiling at her son as she climbed out of her truck. She'd spent hours planning out the remodel for the shop. The place was perfect for what she had in mind, just perfect—oozing country charm, cowboy mystique and simpler times. She could envision shiny belt buckles, bits and bridles in the glass case at the register. The hats and boots along the back wall. Clothing on the left, housewares on the right. Everything cowboy, everything quality and everything unique. With all her contacts from the rodeo circuit, she knew she'd be able to give her patrons the best possible quality. She couldn't wait to get started. "Want to go inside?"

Rowdy shrugged, unbuckling his seat belt. "Sure." He yawned, barely waking up. It had been a long car ride and the kids had been as good as gold. Not a complaint among them. A rarity, really.

"What do you two think?" she asked, opening the back door of her four-door diesel truck. "We can poke around, see how the contractor's doing on the shelving, then go get some breakfast? Then head out to the new place. There'll be plenty of room to run there."

Her niece and nephew looked at her, their lack of interest or enthusiasm no longer surprising her.

"Good, let's go," she said, pulling the store keys from her pocket and climbing onto the wooden porch.

"Can't we eat first?" Otis asked.

"Yeah, I'm hungry, too," Dot added.

"Soon we will," she promised, ignoring the grating tone they used. They tended toward that nasal whine to wear down a person's resistance until they got what they wanted. Poppy refused to buckle. She was excited—hoped they'd get excited, too.

"Chill," Rowdy said, less patient than she was. "You just ate a granola bar and an apple. You're not starving." She placed a hand on his shoulder, not wanting things to escalate between them. Even if he was right.

"So it's true? You're the new owner?" Mr. Cute-Butt Cowboy asked.

She nodded, glancing his way. And stared. *No. No. No. This isn't fair. Not now. Not here. Toben Boone can*not *be here.*

"I had to see it with my own two eyes." He leaned against the doorframe, arms crossed over his broad chest, smiling, dimples showing. "Poppy White. Out of the saddle and—" his eyes traveled over the kids "—domesticated." She stared. Speechless.

She was *responsible*. Domesticated? Why did he make it sound like an insult?

Responsibility was something Toben Boone knew nothing about. Words spun. *So* many words. None of which mattered. Her heart was thumping, but she didn't know if it was caused by anger or surprise or panic.

She glanced at her son, but he had his face pressed against the glass—unaware.

"Morning," she managed, fumbling with the key before opening the door. Rowdy rushed past her and into the shop. Dot and Otis lingered, looking bored, on the wooden plank porch. "Why don't you go look around?" she said to them. "We'll go check out the house after we eat. You can unwind for a while there."

Dot shot her a death glare and Otis sighed before they moved at a glacial pace into the building.

"Those all yours?" Toben asked, watching the two sullen children shuffle inside. His eyebrow cocked up in question.

Damn but he hadn't changed much. He was clean shaven now, but his jaw was covered in stubble. He was still far too easy on the eyes, with his straw hat cocked forward and jeans that fit like a glove. He still had that…charisma. The first time they'd met, she'd sat on her bar stool and watched him in action. He'd been impressive. Whether he was riding a bronc, dancing to George Strait or picking up a woman, he did so with a confidence that drew the eye. And she knew from firsthand experience that he had every right to be confident.

She shook her head. "Rose, my sister's." A sister who needed a vacation, desperately. Nothing like cancer and chemotherapy to realize how precious time was. Rose and Bob had flown to the Bahamas for a romantic two-week getaway, leaving Poppy with their kids. They hadn't met the halfway mark yet and Poppy's patience was fading.

Toben nodded, pushing off the doorframe. He seemed bigger, taking up more space. "What brings you to Stonewall Crossing, Poppy? I never figured you for the small-town shopkeeper sort." He tipped his hat back with his finger and stared down at her with those baby blues.

"Considering how well you knew me?" she asked, refusing to get lost in his eyes. Sure, they'd known of each other on the circuit. But they'd spent ten, maybe twelve, hours together before she'd headed to Santa Fe. And in that time, they hadn't done a lot of talking.

He chuckled. "What I knew, I liked. A hell of a lot."

She smiled reluctantly. Sonofabitch that he was, he still had that boyish charm about him. All dimples, blue eyes and blond curls. Hard not to get sucked in. "I've got things to do."

He nodded. "I'll be seeing you around."

Around? *I hope not.* "Sure." She nodded, stepping inside, and closed the door before he could say anything else.

She leaned against the solid wood for support. It had been seven years since she'd seen Toben Boone. Seven years. A lifetime.

Rowdy's lifetime.

Her gaze fell on her son. Rowdy stood, hands on his hips, inspecting the shop with interest. He was a good boy, inquisitive and patient. A boy who knew who his father was, because Poppy didn't believe in secrets or lies. Rowdy had never met him, had never had the chance—before now. And now…she couldn't bring herself to make the introductions. Her son had his father's dimples and curls—but unlike his father, Rowdy was a good boy, loyal and honest. And since Toben hadn't displayed the least bit of curiosity or interest in finally meeting his son, Poppy wasn't all that eager to rectify the situation.

TOBEN WALKED TO Pop's Bakery, unable to shake the odd sensation in his gut. Seeing Poppy threw him off balance.

"What'll it be?" Carl, the bakery's owner, asked. "Lola made some fresh blueberry muffins. Bear claws? Ham-and-cheese crescent rolls?"

"How about you set me up with a box." Toben smiled, leaning on the counter.

"Feeding the boys at the ranch today?" Carl asked. "Might need more than one."

Toben shook his head. "Figured I'd welcome the new neighbors. Bought out the old hardware store that's been empty for a while."

"The barrel racer?" Carl asked. "Renata was pretty excited to be getting rodeo royalty on Main Street."

Toben nodded. His cousin Renata worked for the city, and she took promoting Stonewall Crossing seriously. There was no doubt Poppy was rodeo royalty. Watching her on her little gray horse had been a thing of beauty. She'd been all business, fluidity and grace, leaning so far forward it was hard to see where horse ended and girl began. Toben had held his breath until they were through the course, mesmerized. Something about her no-nonsense attitude had him twisting for months before he got up the nerve to ask her for a beer.

She'd said no.

"Here ya go." Carl put a large box on the counter. "You make sure and tell her we'd be happy to lend a hand if she needs anything while she's getting settled."

"I will," Toben said, pulling out his wallet from his back pocket.

"Nope." Carl held up his hand. "On the house. Consider it a housewarming gift."

"Housewarming?" Lola, Carl's wife, asked. "Who's moving?"

"No one. Someone just got here. That barrel racer?

Doing the Western-wear shop," Carl said. "Toben's taking breakfast to them."

"Them?" Lola asked. The woman prided herself on knowing everything about everyone in Stonewall Crossing. And new residents meant fresh gossip.

"Just her and her niece and nephews," Toben offered. "Not exactly country kids, from what I could tell."

"Got them gadgets in their hands, all computers, never looking up?" Carl sighed. "Don't understand it."

Lola patted his shoulder. "Times change, sugar. Well, if she's got kids with her, you better tell her about the Fourth of July festivities next month. Most kids still like a parade."

Toben nodded. "Will do."

"You know, it's not a bad idea," Carl said.

Lola and Toben looked at him.

"What are you talking about?" Lola asked.

"A housewarming," Carl said. "Bet Renata'd want to set something up. She was talking about adding more events at the last tourism meeting. A housewarming or welcome to Stonewall might be just the thing."

"Carl, that's a great idea. Bring all the shops on Main Street together," Lola agreed. "I'll get Renata on the phone."

Toben nodded, thanked them again and walked out, carrying the large white box with breakfast treats back around the corner. He nodded at those he passed, drawing in the fresh morning air as he walked. It was mid-June in the Hill Country. The summer was in full swing—sultry nights, floating down the river in an inner tube, campfires and cookouts. Soon enough the town would be crowded with tourists who flocked here for the big Fourth of July festivities. The annual parade, a street carnival and the big Stonewall Crossing rodeo. Other than actual rodeo season, this was his favorite time of year.

And this year Poppy White was here.

Poppy's truck was a monster. It was a giant four-door diesel with a tow package in the bed for pulling horse trailers.

Where was she going to live? There was a small apartment over the shop, but he could guess that wasn't Poppy's style. She'd need to be close to her horses, make sure they had room to roam. They were her family. He'd done a lot of digging, trying to figure her out, years back. And if he remembered right, she didn't have much other family.

He knocked on the shop door and smiled at the boy who opened it.

"Can I help you?" the boy asked, all brash confidence, with boots and a shiny belt buckle.

"Got a breakfast delivery from Pop's Bakery, right around the corner. Welcome to the neighborhood." He held the box out.

The boy smiled and stepped aside so Toben could enter. "Thanks, mister. That's real nice."

Toben smiled back, struck with a hint of recognition. He placed the box on the counter. "There's a lot of nice people in Stonewall Crossing. My family's ranch is here. And they're all good people."

"Rowdy—" Poppy stopped.

"He brought breakfast," the boy said.

"Oh. Thank you." But Poppy's posture was anything but appreciative. She looked…spitting mad.

Guess the shock of seeing him again had worn off and she'd decided to be her old prickly self. Considering last time she'd seen him they'd been tangled naked and drifting off into a well-sated sleep, he'd hoped things would be easier between them. Of course, he'd left before they'd had a chance to talk—hell, he'd left before she'd woken up. A box of welcome pastries might not be enough to wipe the slate clean, but it was a start.

"You a cowboy?" the older, sullen boy asked.

"I'd like to think so," Toben answered.

"If you're a cowboy, where's your horse?" the girl asked, hands on her hips. "Don't *real* cowboys ride horses?"

"Not all the time," Toben responded. "Sometimes they drive a truck, like your aunt. She's a real cowgirl."

The sullen boy sighed and rolled his eyes.

"She's the best," the smaller boy said, smiling at Poppy. "Four-time national champion. Third-fastest barrel-racing time ever. Onetime international champion—"

"Oh my gosh, Rowdy, do we have to hear it again?" the girl asked. "We get it. She's awesome." But her tone was so grating and condescending that Toben bristled.

The younger boy glared at the other two. "You don't get it. Or you'd think it's awesome, too."

Toben agreed. "And deserving of respect." He leveled a hard look at both children.

Poppy placed her hand on the younger boy's shoulder, offering Toben a small smile. "Thanks for bringing food. I'm hoping once they're fed, they'll be a little more civilized."

"Wouldn't that be nice?" Toben shook his head. "Don't thank me. Carl and Lola run the bakery around the corner—Pop's Bakery. It's from them. Also wanted me to tell you the town goes big for Fourth of July. Floats, tubing races and a rodeo—"

"Can we go?" Rowdy asked, excited.

"We'll just have to see." Poppy's hand stroked the boy's cheek. "But I'll do my best."

"There's a table in the back room, Aunt Poppy," the girl said. "I'll put the food in there."

"Thank you, Dot."

"I can't wait for them to go home." Rowdy sighed after the other two had left the room.

"You get to stay longer?" Toben asked.

Poppy shot him a look, her jaw clenched and her posture rigid. What had he said now?

"Nah, we live here now. I'm not going anywhere." The boy grinned up at her. "Well...maybe I'll go get something to eat. Okay, Ma?"

Poppy was a mom? The kid was cute enough to have her genes, that was for sure. But then, Poppy was one of the prettiest women he'd ever seen. He'd heard she was engaged, so maybe she was married now? Or was she raising her son on her own? Surprisingly, he wanted to know.

Poppy grinned at the boy. "Better hurry before they eat it all."

"Thanks again, mister."

Toben tipped his hat at the boy. "No problem."

The boy ran from the room, and Poppy sighed. "Listen, Toben, he hasn't figured out who you are. I mean, he knows your name—I haven't kept anything from him. But...I don't want to spring this on him. I didn't know you'd be here. Are you staying? I mean... We'll make it work if you are." She shook her head. "This doesn't need to be difficult. Just let me tell him you are...*you*. Okay?"

Toben stared at her, her words making no sense. "You lost me."

She glared at him, pure hostility rolling off her tiny frame. "Rowdy knows Toben Boone is his father. But you didn't introduce yourself so he doesn't know *you* are Toben Boone. I'd rather have that conversation with him alone. Like we've been for the last six years."

Toben felt numb all over. "Rowdy?" He swallowed, unable to breathe, to think, to process what the hell she was saying.

"That was Rowdy," she repeated, her irritation mounting. She looked ready to rip into him.

"I don't know what you're talking about, Poppy. But if

you're trying to tell me I'm a…father…" He sucked in a deep breath, his chest hurting so much he pressed a hand over his heart. "Don't you think you waited a little long to tell me I have a son?"

Chapter Two

Poppy hit Ignore on her phone and shoved the pillow she was holding into a newly purchased, newly laundered pillowcase. Mitchell would call back. He always called back. He was reliable—that was one of the reasons she appreciated him. But talking to Mitchell would lead to tears or anger, neither of which she needed right now. She had to figure out how she was going to tell Rowdy that his father was here. And that his father wanted to meet him.

She gritted her teeth and patted the pillow with more force than needed, still trying to wrap her head around Toben's disbelief that morning.

"I told you. I sent you letters. Letter after letter. Left messages with every woman that answered your phone—left messages so you could reach me," she'd said, the remembered humiliation tightening her throat. "And you sent me an autographed picture."

He'd gripped the counter, his hands white-knuckled. "Poppy, come on. You can't honestly believe I'd—"

"Why not? Don't tell me to come on. I was the only woman you hadn't slept with on the circuit. What sort of expectations should I have had of you?" Her whisper rose. She glanced at the door, hoping the kids couldn't hear. She started again, softly, in control. "None. Your picture confirmed it. I wasn't going to lose sleep over it."

"Rowdy is my son?" He stared at her, his jaw tight and his blue eyes raging. "A son I have every right to know."

She was stunned. "Now you want to know him?"

"I didn't know he existed until two minutes ago. If I had, you can be damn sure he'd have had his father in his life. He will now. You tell him and you call me. Tonight." He slammed a business card onto the countertop and stormed out of the shop.

He'd seemed sincerely upset. So much so that she felt a twinge of remorse. No, dammit, she wouldn't feel regret. She'd tried to reach him—again and again. She hadn't wanted to raise Rowdy alone. But Toben had never reached out to her. Was she supposed to have tracked him down so he could tell her to her face he didn't want anything to do with their son?

No. She'd pulled herself up and kept going. She'd had no choice.

"Mom," Rowdy called from down the hall. "Can I paint it black?"

She laughed. "Your room?" she asked.

"Yeah," he answered.

"Um, no. That'd be a little too dark." She shook out the blanket, wincing at the tug in her side. Most days it wasn't so bad, but sometimes when she turned suddenly, there was still pain. Stretching carefully, she finished making up her bed, thankful she'd had the movers unload everything the day before. Moving boxes and clutter aside, it was nice to have their things in one place. The small house already offered the promise of home for her and Rowdy.

"What about orange?" he called.

She left her bedroom and wandered down the hall to the room Rowdy had claimed. He was standing in the middle of the space, hands on his hips, considering.

"Why orange?" she asked. The house needed a lot of work—a lot. But in time they'd make it their own.

"I like orange." He smiled at her.

"I like pink, but I'm not painting my bedroom that color."

He laughed. A flash of Toben sprung to mind. The resemblance between father and son was astonishing. The only difference was Rowdy's hair and eyes—brown like hers, not his father's golden locks and blue eyes.

"Maybe one wall. Maybe. Let's settle in a little first, okay? For now, you'll have to survive with white walls. Maybe orange curtains?" She hugged him. "Where are your cousins?"

"Guest bedroom, watching movies or playing video games or something." He shrugged. "When will Cheeto get here?"

Neither one of them liked to be parted from their horses long. "Mitchell's bringing them up tomorrow," she reminded him.

Rowdy sighed. "He's probably missing me."

"I know he is." Her son loved his pony. And his pony loved him right back. He followed Rowdy all over, more like a dog than the sturdy spotted pony he was. "You got a minute?" she asked.

He nodded. "Shoot."

She smiled. "Well, I'm not sure how to tell you this. So I'm just gonna say it, okay?"

"You and Mitchell are getting married?" he asked, a slight frown on his face.

"What? Why would you think that?"

"You were gonna marry him. Dot says he still wants to marry you," he said. "Real bad. That's why he's always around."

"And he knows I don't want to get married. Ever. To anyone. He's my best friend, that's all." She waited.

"I feel bad for him, Ma." Rowdy stared up at her.

"Oh, well, if you feel bad for him, then I'll marry him," she teased.

Rowdy laughed. "I don't want you to marry him. I like him but…"

Exactly. She liked him, valued his friendship, but there was no spark there. She and Mitchell had tried, hoping their friendship could grow into something more. But his proposal had been prompted by her pregnancy and Mitchell's goodness. His wife had just left him, and he'd been devastated and grieving. And Poppy had needed help. They'd realized it was a mistake a few months later. But instead of losing a fiancé, she'd gained a best friend—one who told it like it was, one she could call if she needed help or share a beer with at the end of a long day. He'd been a fixture since before Rowdy was born. As her friend, nothing more.

She sank onto the corner of his bed, putting thoughts of Mitchell aside. She took a deep breath, smiled and said, "No, what I want to talk about has nothing to do with Mitchell."

"Okay," he said, sitting beside her.

"I've told you a little about your dad," she said, her throat constricting.

"Toben Boone." He smiled up at her.

"Well…" She tucked one of his curls behind his ear. She couldn't say it… The words stuck in her throat.

"He okay?" Rowdy asked, his brown eyes going wide with concern. "Something happen to him?"

"No, no." She shook her head. "He's here."

Rowdy jumped up. "Here? In Stonewall Crossing? Is that why we moved here?"

"I didn't know he was here. I lost track of him a while back." Because she'd stopped looking for him, stopped hoping he'd change his mind and want to meet his son.

"Does he know I'm here? Have you talked to him?" Rowdy was so excited he was practically bouncing.

"I have. And so have you," she said. "The man today with the pastries. That was him."

Rowdy stared at her. His smile faded, the energy seeming to slowly drain from his body. "Why didn't he say anything to me?" His shoulders slumped.

She reached for him and pulled him close before continuing. "Toben said he didn't know about you, Rowdy."

Rowdy was rigid in her arms. "You told him."

"I did," she agreed.

"So he's lying?"

"I'm not sure," she said, continuing to hug him. "I don't know what happened. But he does want to meet you."

Rowdy stepped out of her arms and looked at her, the excitement returning to his eyes. "He does?"

She nodded, her stomach knotting.

"When?"

"What do you think about having him over?" she asked.

Rowdy glanced across the hall at the closed bedroom door. "But Dot. And Otis." He wrinkled his nose. "I want him to like me."

"Of course he will like you, Rowdy." She tried to smile, tried to sound optimistic instead of terrified. "If your cousins are underfoot, it'll be that much more obvious that you're awesome."

Rowdy laughed.

"What do you think?" she asked.

Rowdy shrugged. "Okay."

"Okay," she said, taking Toben's card from her pocket. "He wanted me to call him when I'd talked to you. Today."

Rowdy smiled. "I'm glad he wants to meet me. I've got lots to tell him."

Poppy swallowed, fighting back tears. "You do." She

stood, eager to put some distance between them. She didn't like upsetting Rowdy or getting too emotional in front of him. He was a kid, and while she believed in full disclosure, she was very aware of how things were presented. Rowdy would grow up soon enough, without her putting adult worries on his shoulders. "Need anything?" she asked.

He shrugged. "When's school start?" he asked.

"It's only June," she answered. Rowdy loved school. "You'll have to suffer through a few more weeks of freedom with me."

He nodded. "Got time to get Cheeto settled," he said, opening a box. "And paint the wall orange." He shot her a grin.

Poppy chuckled and left him, the wooden floor of the hallway creaking loudly. She stopped walking; the squeaking stopped. The floors might take top priority. She took Toben's card into her bedroom and lay on the bed, staring up at the ceiling. She could do this. She didn't need to worry—Toben just wanted to meet his son. Something he had every right to do. Something she'd wanted for Rowdy in the beginning. Back then she'd hoped Rowdy would tame Toben Boone—show him it was time to grow up and why. But now she knew even less about the man than before. And this man, this stranger, wanted to spend time with her son.

Toben checked his phone again. Still nothing. It was almost six. She hadn't called.

"What's eating you?" his cousin Deacon asked, swinging the saddle back onto the rack. "You planning to help or are you going to keep standing there staring at your damn phone?"

Toben tucked the phone into his pocket and focused on the task at hand. Once the saddles were stowed, they brushed the horses down, removing any thorns or stickers from their coats and tails. Toben ran his hand down the back of the dapple-gray horse's left leg. The horse shifted, letting Toben cup the hoof. He used the hoof pick, removing mud and rocks that might bruise the horse and affect its gait. He'd just finished all four hooves when his phone rang.

"Toben here," he said, stepping away from his cousin and the horses.

"It's Poppy." She sounded out of breath. "Would you like to come to dinner with us?"

His anger was instantaneous. "I just want to spend time with *Rowdy*." He wasn't sure he wanted to spend time with her. He didn't want to believe she'd keep the boy from him but... How could she have gone so long without telling him?

"If you want to see him, you have to see me," she returned. "I don't play games, Toben. Not with my son. You're a stranger to me and to him."

"Because of you," he argued, his tone hard. "I want to see my son." He heard a *thunk* and a muffled "Shit" behind him but didn't turn. "You've had him for six years. I've known about him for four hours."

"Then come to dinner." She paused. "He wants you to come."

Toben closed his eyes, resting his forehead on the top rail of the stall in front of him. "He does?"

"Yes, he does." Her voice wavered.

"What's he like, Poppy? What's his favorite thing?" he asked. "Does he ride? Like horses?"

"He grew up on fairgrounds and in rodeo arenas. He could ride blindfolded, knows all the rules of every event, knows all my stats. And yours."

He smiled. At least Rowdy knew who he was. That was something. But it didn't ease the hurt he felt, the sharp, cutting pain in his chest. "What time?"

"Dinner is at seven thirty," she said. "But you're welcome anytime." He could tell it was hard for her to say those words. Maybe she wasn't any happier about this than he was. Well, if she could try, so could he. For Rowdy's sake, he'd mind his temper and try to be some sort of father figure. Whatever the hell that meant.

"Should I bring anything?" he asked, more than a little worried.

"Just yourself. We'll see you then," she said and hung up.

Toben stayed where he was, the anger and hurt, joy and loss that churned his insides making him unsteady on his feet.

"You okay?" Deacon asked again, without the heat this time. "'Cause it sounds like you've got a hell of a lot to tell me."

Toben pushed off the fence and turned, shoving his phone into his pocket. "It's been a hell of a day."

Toben stood by while Deacon finished the horse's hooves. He knew he was being a useless fool, but he was in shock— all over again.

When Deacon had turned the horses into their stalls and put the equipment away, Toben followed him from the barn. His gaze traveled over the pens and down the fence line, noting the lights of the Lodge blazing. The Boone Ranch belonged to his uncle Teddy. It was a massive spread that tracked their white-tail deer and exotic-game numbers, housed a large horse refuge, turned a profit raising cattle and ran a top-of-the-line bed-and-breakfast. The Lodge offered down-home cooking, hayrides, horse rides, star tours and bonfires complete with sing-alongs. From the look of it, it was going to be a busy weekend. Business as usual.

But nothing felt usual to Toben.

"Start talking," Deacon prodded.

"You remember Poppy White?" Toben asked. "Barrel racer?"

Deacon nodded. "How could I forget? You ran from her so fast you left skid marks. Yeah, I remember her. And you being all hangdog for months after."

"I… We have a son." The word felt strange on his tongue.

Deacon stopped walking and faced him. "A son?" His smile was wide and anguished.

"Shit, man, I'm sorry," Toben murmured. Deacon's family was killed a few years before, leaving Deacon sadder and a lot more isolated than a man should ever be. Toben hated seeing pain in his cousin's eyes.

"We're not talking about my life, Toben. We're talking about yours."

Toben nodded.

"Why didn't she tell you? I'd be so pissed—"

"She said she tried." He shook his head. "I'm plenty pissed but…I have a son. And being pissed at his mother, the person he knows and loves best, would be a big mistake on my part."

Deacon blew out a slow breath. "What are you going to do?"

"Go to dinner," he answered. "Sit across the table and try not to stare at him."

"What's his name?" Deacon asked.

Toben grinned. "Rowdy."

"That sounds like your son." Deacon laughed. "So he's about six?"

It had been seven years since his night with Poppy. He nodded. "Guess so. I don't even know his birthday. He's a good boy, though. From the little I saw of him today."

"Better clean up," Deacon said, sweeping Toben with a head-to-toe inspection. "Take some ice cream or a pie. Think Clara was making pies earlier."

Toben nodded. Pie was good. Boys loved pie. And he wanted to make his boy happy. He wanted to know what made him smile and laugh, what his favorite color was, what he wanted to be when he grew up...everything. He hoped Poppy would realize he had the right to know these things. He couldn't shake the feeling that she'd kept Rowdy from him. And that feeling left a nasty, bitter taste in the back of his throat.

Chapter Three

The smoke detector was beeping loudly. Dot was screaming and Rowdy was trying to help find the broom. Poppy stood on the stool, waving packing paper at the smoke detector, hoping the beeping—and the screaming—would stop. The old stove had started smoking as soon as she turned it on. She'd opened the windows and turned on the Vent-A-Hood, but the smoke had still triggered the smoke detector.

"Got it." Rowdy held the broom up to her.

"Thanks." She stood on tiptoe, trying to press the reset button with the tiny hook on the end of the broom handle. But the ceiling was high and Poppy's five feet two inches could stretch only so far. She leaned forward, teetered on the stool and fell.

"Gotcha." Toben's arms caught her, preventing her from crashing to the wood floor. "Need a hand?"

He smelled like heaven, even in a smoky kitchen. And his arms, solid and thick, held her as if she weighed nothing. His blue eyes crashed into hers, making her breathless, weightless…and an idiot. As soon as her feet hit the floor, she shrugged out of his arms and stepped back. "Um…" He was handsome—big deal. She wasn't some young, needy thing—not anymore.

"She can't reach the reset button," Rowdy volunteered loudly.

Toben nodded at Rowdy, grinned and took the broom from Poppy. He tapped the button and the room—the kids—fell silent. The cooking element made an ominous sizzle-pop sound, making Poppy suspect the stove might just take precedence over the squeaky floors.

"My ears are ringing," Dot whined. "It hurts."

"You're such a baby," Otis snapped. "Get over it."

"You two can set the table." She spoke calmly, ignoring the exchange.

Dot's response came quickly. "Why do we have to—"

"Because I asked you to," she said, her tone never fluctuating. "Thank you. Rowdy, can you see what our guest would like to drink?"

She saw her son's quick glance at Toben, the bright red patches coloring his cheeks. Her boy was nervous. She looked Toben's way, hoping he'd see his son's discomfort. But...Toben looked exactly the same as Rowdy. Red cheeked, nervous, uncertain.

"Sure," Rowdy said. "Want something to drink?"

"Iced tea?" Toben asked.

"Sweet or unsweet?" Rowdy nodded. "There's only one right answer."

She laughed. So did Toben.

"Sweet," Toben said.

Rowdy nodded. "Yep."

Toben looked at her, his smile fading, to be replaced by something else. Anger? Sadness? She didn't know. She didn't know how to read this man. Not that it mattered. They were going to have to figure this out—together.

"Dinner is edible," she assured him. "Must have been something on the cooking element and the place started smoking."

"I brought dessert," he said, pointing at a pie in the center of the table.

"You cook?" Rowdy asked.

"You made this?" Otis asked. "I'm not eating it. Who are you?"

"Why is he here, Aunt Poppy?" Dot asked.

"Mr. Boone is a friend of mine," Poppy said. "We used to rodeo together."

"And he's my dad," Rowdy said. The smile he shot Toben made Poppy's heart melt. Pure, honest, sweet and so full of love.

Toben was equally affected. He nodded at Rowdy. "I am."

"Huh," Otis said. "You do look like him. Wow. You look just like him."

"You've got Aunt Poppy's hair color. And her brown eyes," Dot argued. "But yeah, other than that."

"Good thing I'm a good-looking guy," Toben said, winking at Rowdy.

Rowdy's laugh filled the room.

"So you two weren't married?" Dot asked. "That's wrong."

"Mom and Dad say you're not supposed to do…that… until after you're married," Otis offered, poking the pie with a fork as he set the table.

"And they're right," Poppy agreed, tension mounting.

"So you were married?" Otis pushed.

"Did you make fried chicken?" Toben asked. "It smells like fried chicken."

"She did." Rowdy nodded. "It's my favorite."

"Mine, too," Toben agreed, his blue eyes never leaving Rowdy.

Dinner went well. She and Toben did their best to keep conversation from getting too awkward. Which meant preventing Dot and Otis from saying too much. Her niece was almost twelve and Otis was ten, and they knew just enough to make things awkward fairly often. But once dinner was over and she was loading plates into the rickety dishwasher, Rowdy asked, "Can we go for a walk? Just me and…my dad?"

"You…" She broke off. "Where?"

"The barn and back?" Rowdy suggested. "I can show him where Cheeto and Stormy will live."

She wiped her hands on the dish towel, hoping it hid her shaking. "Sure."

"We can have pie when we get back?" Rowdy asked, looking up at Toben.

"Toben might have to go. Work starts early on a ranch—"

"Pie after sounds good," Toben interrupted, not looking at her.

"I want ice cream," Otis chimed in.

Poppy stared at her sister's children, disappointed in their lack of manners. "Ice cream, sure. Feel like playing a board game?"

They looked at her like she was the crazy one.

"No?" she asked. "Okay."

"I'll play when we get back, Mom," Rowdy said, walking out of the kitchen.

Poppy served Dot and Otis ice cream, washed the dinner dishes and half-heartedly unpacked a box—her gaze drifting out the window again and again to see Toben and Rowdy side by side. Plaid shirts, straw cowboy hats, well-worn leather cowboy boots and polished belt buckles. But it was more than their matching getups. Her boy was the mirror image of the man.

And she didn't know how she felt about that.

Then her attention wandered to Toben Boone's delectable rear. Those jeans. That butt. It was quite a view. She scrubbed the skillet with renewed vigor.

"Aunt Poppy, can we call Mom?" Dot asked. "I miss her."

"I'm sure she's missing you, too," Poppy agreed. "You can call her."

"Okay," Dot said, slipping from the table, leaving half of her ice cream untouched and hurrying to the guest bedroom.

"If she's not going to eat it." Otis pulled his sister's bowl closer.

"Is there anything you'd like to do, Otis, now that we're here?" she asked, sitting across the table from him. "The river's at the bottom of the hill. We could go tubing." If the water was up. Considering how hot it had been this afternoon, she'd sit in a puddle if it helped cool things off.

He frowned at her. "Tubing?"

"Float down the river," she explained. "In an inner tube."

"Why would we do that?" He spooned ice cream into his mouth. "Isn't there a pool?"

She stood again and peered out the window. Rowdy and Toben were almost to the barn. "No, there's no pool here." Why would she and Rowdy need a pool when the Medina River was practically in their backyard?

"Man, this place stinks." His spoon clattered in his bowl.

By the time she'd turned around, Otis had joined Dot in the guest room, the floor squeaking with each step. So the house needed more work than she'd realized. But it didn't stink. She eyed the stove. Okay, maybe it did stink a little. She wiped down the kitchen counter, trying not to stare out the window.

Her phone rang. "Hello?"

"Hey, Pops." Mitchell's voice was low and soothing.

"Hey, Mitchell, what's up?"

"Figured I'd check on you all. See if Rowdy's packed his cousins into an empty moving box and shipped them to Australia or something."

She laughed. "No. They're bigger than him, you know?"

"And slower," he argued. "How's it going?"

She pushed through the front screen door and sat on the porch swing, sighing. "You wouldn't believe me if I told you."

"Shoot," he said.

"No, not right now. I'm too tired." She yawned.

"You sound it. I'll be up tomorrow with your babies," he said. "How's the town? Land? Just as pretty as the pictures looked?"

Her eyes wandered along the horizon, feathered clouds of cotton-candy pink and vibrant purple streaking across the sky. She stood, perched on the wraparound porch railing, leaning against the thick carved pillar, and stared out over the rolling hills dotted with stubby cedar trees. Sprawling Spanish oaks blew in the evening breeze, a calming sound that eased some of the knots from her shoulders. Rocky outcrops dotted the ground, adding to the rugged beauty of the land. Beyond the clumps of prickly cactus and thistle, Poppy spied the perfect place for a vegetable garden. She had plans for this place—saw a future here for her and Rowdy. "The house is rough but…the property? It's gorgeous. Prettier than the pictures. I'd have paid a hell of a lot more than what we settled on."

"That pretty?" He chuckled. "What's Rowdy think?"

She paused, glancing toward the barn. Rowdy and Toben were talking. Rather, Rowdy was talking, and Toben was listening—wearing a beautiful smile. Her heart twisted sharply, a flare of warning tightening her stomach. Rowdy was her everything. Keeping him safe and happy was her only goal now. She just hadn't figured on Toben Boone being involved. "He seems pretty happy at the moment." She only hoped Toben's interest wasn't some passing notion. That once the newness of being a father, of having a son, wore off, he wouldn't break Rowdy's heart.

"YOU WERE AN ALL-AROUND?" Rowdy asked.

Toben nodded. In his day, he'd competed in all the rodeo events. And won a pretty penny and more than his fair share of belt buckles in the process. "Used to be. Now only if it's something I really want to do. A bull or bronc I feel I need to ride. You want to rodeo?"

Rowdy smiled. "Not sure. It's dangerous sometimes."

He nodded. "True. You have to be careful. Have good instincts."

"Ma said her daddy was both and he still ended up dying in the arena." Rowdy frowned. "She saw it."

Toben had grown up hearing about Barron White— anyone related to rodeo had. The man was a legend, a true ambassador for the sport. Toben had been at the Houston rodeo the day the man had died, but he hadn't seen it. To hear about it was bad enough. He glanced at the house, his heart aching for Poppy. She'd seen her daddy gored, trampled in the dirt and dragged from the arena.

"What about your dad?" Rowdy asked.

"Don't know who he was," Toben admitted. He looked at the boy, wishing it weren't true.

"Why?"

Toben chuckled. "My mother won't tell me."

"She doesn't know?"

Rowdy was too young to realize how painful that question was. He meant no offense. But the truth of it stung. "Nope."

Rowdy nodded. "Sorry."

Toben placed his hand on Rowdy's shoulder. "No reason. I've got plenty of family to keep me in line."

"It's always been me and Mom." There was no bitterness or sadness, just fact. But his son's words stoked Toben's anger. Rowdy was a Boone. He had a family, a big one at that. Something else Poppy'd kept from him.

Rowdy picked up a stick, whacking the thistle flowers as they ambled back down the road. "Aunt Rose comes around now and then but they don't get along for long."

"Dot and Otis's mom?" Toben asked. If the kids were anything like their parents, Toben could easily understand why Poppy and Rose weren't close.

"Yeah, Aunt Rose and Uncle Bob." He whacked another thistle. "Uncle Bob's nice. He always has candy in his pocket. Mitchell, too. Mitchell's always around, helping me and Ma. He's real funny."

Mitchell? Who the hell was Mitchell? What did *always around* mean, exactly? But then, Poppy was a beautiful woman. It made sense for her to have a man in her life. A man in Rowdy's life. His anger and frustration pressed hot and heavy against his chest. They were almost to the house and Toben realized he had at least a hundred questions he hadn't asked. He'd have to make sure they had more time together—soon.

"Good walk?" Poppy asked, curled up on the front porch swing. Toben tried not to stare into her big brown eyes. Instead he focused on her long brown hair, braided over one shoulder. She wore jeans and a short-sleeved blue blouse, her scuffed and worn boots used for work—not for show. She wasn't about making impressions or putting on airs, he'd always admired that about her. She was Poppy, take her or leave her. The same woman she'd been years ago. The same woman who'd turned his world on its head, put longing in his heart and made him run for the hills.

The mother of his son.

His anger warmed him—and helped him keep his guard up.

"Yep," Rowdy said, sliding into the swing beside her. "Wish Cheeto was here. Maybe we can go for a ride when he gets here?" he asked Toben.

"Good idea," Toben agreed, leaning against the porch railing. "Or you two could come out to the ranch tomorrow. I live there, on the Boone Ranch. Work there, too. We've got a lot of horses on the place, and the food's good. Give you a break from cooking. And setting off smoke detectors." He couldn't stop his teasing smile.

When she smiled back at him, every inch of him responded.

"I don't think Dot and Otis are big horse lovers." She frowned at Rowdy. "They're leaving soon, though."

"Not soon enough," Rowdy grumbled.

He saw that she tried not to laugh but failed. It was the sweetest sound. Free and easy. Like their son. He liked it.

"They're not the most…agreeable kids, are they?" Toben asked, chuckling. They were a stark contrast to Rowdy, one he was suddenly very thankful to Poppy for. Not that he was ready to feel thankful to her. Not yet.

She shook her head. "When Rose got cancer, everyone just sort of gave them what they wanted to try to cheer them up. Now nothing seems to really make them happy."

Toben nodded. "She better?" he asked. "Your sister?"

"Yes, much better."

"Cancer's a bitch." He paused, staring at Rowdy, then Poppy. "That just sort of slipped out."

She nodded at him, her brow arching. "It happens. And, since we're talking about cancer, I'm fine with it."

He grinned.

"I'll get you both some pie," she offered, disappearing into the house before he could answer.

They all sat on the porch swing, enjoying Clara's apple pie and the company.

"Can we visit tomorrow night?" Rowdy asked. "Beats sitting at home and watching them play video games."

Toben looked at Poppy over Rowdy's head. He saw the

indecision on her face, the nervousness. What was she worrying over? Considering how quickly this had come to light, he thought he'd been handling things pretty well. But...it was new for them all. And if he was smart, he wouldn't start pushing for more time with Rowdy. Yet.

"It's an open invitation. All you have to do is call, Poppy. And thanks for dinner." His voice was soft. "For this evening." He meant it.

Her gaze met his then. He couldn't look away, didn't want to. She was damn beautiful—the mother of his son. A boy he was well on his way to loving. A boy she'd kept from him... His anger tightened his jaw, but her brown eyes held him captive. The longer he stared, the more her wariness faded. And in its place he caught a flash of the fiery woman he'd loved for one night. The woman he'd never quite gotten over.

Chapter Four

"What do you mean, he's here?" Mitchell stared down at her, hands on his hips, wearing a dazed expression. Poppy had waited to share the news of Toben's appearance until they were near the barn, away from the house and Rowdy.

She knew exactly what was going through his mind—Mitchell had that sort of face. One of the many reasons she'd never let him get pulled into a poker game: he'd lose his shirt. His openness was something Poppy had always respected about the man. That and his reliability.

"Does he live here?" Mitchell asked, tipping his cowboy hat back on his head. "I mean…hell, Poppy, are you okay with…this?"

"No." She shrugged. "I don't know." She'd spent a lot of time wondering that same thing. How had she ended up here? Never in her wildest dreams had she thought they'd end up neighbors. But giving up on something—quitting—wasn't in her. "I'm still reeling."

Mitchell blew out a long, slow breath. "And Rowdy?" He shook his head. "After all this time he comes by with *pie* and wants to play house? I'm not a fightin' man, but, damn, I'd like to knock that sonofabitch on his ass and—"

"Mitchell!" Rowdy came barreling down the fence line, all smiles.

"Still in your pj's?" Mitchell squatted by her son, catching him in a hug. "Sleep good?"

Rowdy shook his head. "Couldn't sleep. Dot and Otis were arguing over their game. And the house...makes noises."

Poppy glanced back at the house. "We'll set up the guest rooms today. That way you have your room to yourself and Mitchell's not stuck on the couch, okay?" Since she couldn't fix the noises right away—she needed to find a repairman. Soon.

Rowdy nodded, yawning widely. "Sounds like a plan, Ma."

"How about some pancakes?" Mitchell asked. "I'm starved."

"Not sure the stove can handle pancakes," Poppy admitted. "Might not be a bad idea to replace most of the appliances in the place."

"Saw a little restaurant on the square." Mitchell glanced at his watch. "Bet we could get some breakfast grub before they stop serving. If you can find some clothes, of course."

Rowdy's head turned right, then left. "Okay, but where is—"

"They're in the barn, Rowdy. Mitchell and I got them situated but you can go say hi real quick," Poppy interrupted. "We'll go for a ride after breakfast, okay?"

Rowdy dashed toward the barn, grinning. She was still smiling when she looked at Mitchell. In an instant her smile was gone. The man was staring at her, hard.

"What?" she asked, concerned.

"I don't trust him," he said, his voice low.

Poppy's throat felt tight. She didn't either.

"I've been with you and Rowdy through...everything. Don't expect me to be all right with this asshole just showing up. Can't do it." He shook his head. "What's his plan? What does he want?"

She stepped forward, placing her hand on his arm. "I don't know. We haven't exactly talked things through yet." Something she'd rectify soon. She patted his arm. "For the record, I'm not fine with it either. But what can I do?"

He glanced at her, then at her hand on his arm.

She took a step back and shook her head. "I don't like the look on your face, Mitchell Lee. So stop it. I'm going to wake my sister's monsters so we can go eat." She headed back toward the house, hoping Otis and Dot were already moving. They seemed to prefer staying up and sleeping in—the exact opposite of her and Rowdy's schedule. "I thought you were coming in tonight," she called back over her shoulder.

"Yeah, well... Poppy," Mitchell called out, stopping her. "I like the place."

She nodded, smiling. "Me, too."

Dot and Otis were up, fighting over the sink and the toothpaste, the dripping faucet...even the towel. Poppy ignored their bickering, trying not to worry about whatever Mitchell's look meant. And Rowdy. In the last twenty-four hours, Poppy's level of anxiety had quadrupled. She wasn't a worrier; she was a doer. But she didn't know what to *do* about this situation.

"Why can't we just eat cereal?" Otis asked. "It's too early to go out."

"It's nine, Otis," Poppy said. "And I don't have any cereal. So we go out or you go hungry."

"Figures," Dot murmured. "Way to be prepared."

Poppy shot her niece a look. "We'll be more prepared when you help me shop later, Dot."

Dot's eyes narrowed and her lips flattened, but she didn't say anything.

"Who's ready?" Mitchell asked, standing in the doorway.

"I am," Rowdy answered. "Starving."

Poppy followed them outside, reminding herself that she was the grown-up and she needed to keep her temper in check. Dot and Otis's life had been tough the last year. She knew how difficult it was to see your mom waste away. It took a toll on children, made them harder. But Dot and Otis were lucky, Rose was getting stronger every day. Until their family was reunited, Poppy would continue to be calm and consistent with her niece and nephew—not lose her cool even though *she* was on edge.

They loaded into her truck, buckled in and drove out the gate of the small ranch she already thought of as home. She listened to Rowdy and Mitchell's banter as they drove along the winding back roads, admiring the picturesque hills, cedar and stone fences, and lazily grazing cattle. This was beautiful country.

A few homesteads cropped up as they drew closer to town.

Turn-of-the-century homes. Church turrets. A city park with a grand gazebo. Then Main Street led into town square. Stonewall Crossing had a grand courthouse, surrounded by old oak and pecan trees and carved benches. It was charming and, according to the property agent who had found the ranch for her, a tourist treasure. She drove along Main Street until they reached Pop's Bakery. The town was already bustling, making parking scarce.

"Looks crowded," Mitchell said. "Good sign."

She parked, smiling as Rowdy bounced out of the truck and toward the shop. Otis and Dot seemed to perk up, too, following Rowdy without dragging their feet.

The smell of cinnamon, coffee and bacon greeted them. Poppy's stomach growled.

"Hungry?" Mitchell asked, chuckling.

She nodded. She hadn't eaten much last night.

"Me, too," Mitchell said. "There's a table over there."

He grabbed her hand and tugged her to the table against the far wall.

She went, returning the smiles and nods of the curious residents of Stonewall Crossing. She was curious about them, too. They'd just been seated when a woman approached the table. Tall and blonde, she had bright eyes and an engaging smile.

"Poppy White? Welcome to Stonewall Crossing." She stuck out her hand. "Renata Boone."

Poppy felt the blood drain from her face. "Renata Boone?" She shook the woman's hand. A glance at Rowdy told her he'd missed the exchange.

"You can't take five steps without running into a Boone in Stonewall Crossing." An older man joined them. "Carl Stephens, owner of this fine bakery. How you settling in at the old Travis place?"

"Gorgeous country," Mitchell offered.

Poppy nodded, processing Mr. Stephens's comments. "There's some work to be done."

"Ma's got big plans," Rowdy said. "She doesn't mind work."

"This is my son, Rowdy. My niece, Dot, nephew, Otis, and Mitchell Lee." She ruffled Rowdy's hair.

"I don't mean to interrupt your breakfast," Renata said, her attention wandering around the table. "But I'd love to talk to you about participating in the Fourth of July festivities. And rodeo, of course. Maybe even riding in the Grand Entry? It's a pretty big deal, as you know. Might be a good way to open your shop, if it's ready by then?" She paused, pulling a card from her pocket. "Anyway, I'd love to visit with you."

Poppy read the card. Renata Boone, Stonewall Crossing, Director of Tourism. Regardless of who or what she might be to Toben, Poppy needed to make a place for herself here. And Renata Boone would have the connections to make that happen. She smiled at the woman, adding a sincere, "I'd like that, thank you."

"Taking some *kolaches* to the guys?" Mr. Stephens asked Renata.

Renata nodded. "Bottomless pits, every single one of them. You know that old saying, the way to a man's heart is through his stomach? Pretty much true of every Boone I know." She waved before heading to the counter, collecting her box and leaving the bakery, a little bell ringing as the door closed behind her.

"Take a gander at the menu, I'll be back to take your order." Mr. Stephens offered them menus before heading to another table.

Poppy took one, but her focus remained on the pretty blonde woman walking down the cobblestoned sidewalk until she disappeared around the corner. She was a Boone. But where did she fit?

"Ma, can we get pancakes and bacon?" Rowdy asked, drawing her attention.

"Sure," she agreed. "Sounds good to me, too."

"Make that three," Mitchell joined in. "Extra pancakes. And bacon."

Rowdy laughed, using Mitchell's favorite joke. "Gotta fill up both legs?"

"You know it," Mitchell agreed.

Poppy watched the two of them with a smile.

Mr. Stephens returned, his pen hovering over a small notepad. "What'll it be?"

"I want some grapefruit," Dot piped up. "Or a cantaloupe and cottage cheese."

Carl Stephens scratched his head. "A grapefruit I can do—I think."

Dot sighed, dropping her menu on the table.

"You want a grapefruit over pancakes?" Otis shook his head. "Not me."

Poppy grinned, watching Dot's expression waver. Why was she pushing so hard? Determined to be so damn disagreeable?

"The pancakes are real good," Mr. Stephens said. "And we've got some fresh strawberries I can put on top, if you like."

Dot looked at the older man, smiling slightly. "Yes, thank you."

Poppy breathed a sigh of relief, finishing their order.

"Oh, and coffee," Mitchell added. "Lots and lots of coffee. Please."

"I can do that." Mr. Stephens smiled, collected the menus and headed back to the counter.

"Well, everyone seems nice enough," Mitchell said, nodding at the two men at the table opposite them.

Poppy nodded, trying—and failing—to dismiss Renata Boone's connection to the Boone family. It had been seven years, give or take a few months. It was possible Toben had finally met someone he wanted to settle down with.

She glanced at Rowdy.

For all she knew, Toben was married with kids. Rowdy might have brothers and sisters. She and Toben needed to talk. "When are you thinking of opening the store?" Mitchell asked, effectively redirecting her line of thought.

She shot him a grateful smile. "The sooner, the better. With the Fourth on the horizon, makes sense to have the place open. It's in decent shape, really. I can take you over—"

"Not again." Otis sighed. "We spent hours there yesterday."

"You're playing your game, anyway," Rowdy pointed out. "You can do that anywhere."

"I'd like to see the shop," Mitchell said.

But Poppy had made her son a promise and she made a point of never breaking them. "Maybe. After we take the horses out for a ride."

Dot and Otis moaned, but it didn't matter. Rowdy was smiling ear to ear.

TOBEN NODDED AS his cousin Renata slid a big box of pastries onto the long table. He poured himself another cup of steaming coffee and sat in the break room off the ranch offices. Considering the ground he had to cover today, he needed more coffee—and some of whatever Renata just carried in.

"You're looking a little bleary-eyed, Toben." She patted him on the arm. "No worries—I brought food to help start things on the right foot. My brothers around?"

He nodded, sipping his coffee as he peered into the box of breakfast treats. "Hunter's in the office. Fisher's at the vet hospital today." The sound of crunching gravel and the roar of a diesel engine drew his eye to the front window. "Looks like Archer's truck just pulled up." He bit back a curse and swallowed his coffee. It was too early for Archer. He and his cousin, a know-it-all sonofabitch, didn't always see eye to eye. Yes, Archer was better now that he had Eden and the girls. But when it came to work, he was still the same old insufferable ass he'd always been.

"Pull an all-nighter?" she asked, smiling.

"I wish," he mumbled, taking a hearty bite out of a sausage pastry.

"Don't tell me Toben Boone was turned down." Renata sat in the chair beside him.

He shook his head and rested his elbows on the long wooden table. After he'd forced himself to leave Poppy's place, he'd been unable to sleep. He replayed every second with his son—over and over. He lay in his bunk, his mind racing with questions he wanted answered. Stupid things like Rowdy's bedtime routine. Did he have one, growing up on the circuit? What was his favorite food? He'd said he liked pie but Toben didn't know if he was being polite or honest. Did he like rope tricks? Know how to play horseshoes? Was he left-handed, like Toben was?

He wanted to know more. To see more.

Rowdy's smile. His laugh. He was a fine boy. Poppy had done a good job.

But once he started thinking about Poppy, things got mixed up. It'd be easier if she weren't…Poppy. But she was. She was the same. And now she was the mother of his son. And while he was undeniably proud of his son, Poppy's part in this turn of events was a raw and open wound.

He slammed his coffee cup down on the table with unexpected force.

"Still stewing?" Deacon asked, entering the break room and pouring himself a cup of coffee. Archer trailed behind.

"Hush," Renata said. "I don't know what's eating him, but it's too early to pick. Be nice, boys."

Toben shot his cousin a grin, accepting the kiss she pressed to his temple.

"Archer, I have an idea," Renata said. "I know it's early, but I met Poppy White at Pop's Bakery today and she might be someone to bring in for next summer's riding camp. We could finally have an advanced camp, see if she'd agree to teach some tricks, maybe even consider some one-on-one training for future barrel racers?"

Toben sat back in his chair. Here he was hoping he'd catch a break. Couldn't a man eat his breakfast in peace? He glanced at Archer—curious to hear what his prickly cousin would have to say.

"Poppy who?" Archer asked.

"White." Renata rolled her eyes. "She's rodeo royalty, someone that could help the refuge."

"Why would she want to?" Archer asked, pouring himself some coffee.

"She has a son." Renata leaned against the counter. "Well-spoken little guy, all manners and smiles. Made me think she might be good with kids."

Toben was grinning as he stared into his coffee cup. She'd described Rowdy to a T. His boy did have manners. And a smile—his mama's smile. His grin faded.

"Guess so. If Toben's okay with it?" Archer asked, peering into the pastry box.

Toben sat up then, leveling a hard stare at Deacon. "Really?" Archer knew? *Shit.*

Deacon held up his hands. "He heard us talking."

Archer looked back and forth between them, one brow arching high. "What?"

"I'm missing something." Renata pushed off the counter, her attention bouncing between the three of them. "What's going on?"

Archer and Deacon stared at him, clearly intending for him to be the one to share the news.

"You don't like her?" Renata asked. "I guess you know her from your rodeo days? She seemed perfectly nice to me. So did her son and fella. Good-looking guy and a real cute family—"

Toben stood so fast he bumped his coffee cup onto the floor. He shook his head, mumbling a curse as he hunted down some paper towels. He knew they were watching him, knew he was making a jackass out of himself and knew there wasn't a damn thing he could do about it.

So her boyfriend was here, the one Rowdy had mentioned? So what? Shouldn't matter. He shouldn't care. It didn't change the fact that Rowdy was his son... He needed to make sure Poppy's fella understood that. He finished wiping up his mess and put the coffee cup in the sink, his chest heavy.

He was a near perfect stranger to his son. Apparently this man wasn't. He got to have breakfast with him. Might even have the chance to put him to bed. His grip on the counter tightened.

"Toben?" Renata's voice was concerned. "I'm really sorry. I'm not sure what's going on, but I didn't mean to get you all riled up."

He shook his head, taking his time before he turned to face them. When he did, he tried his best to keep his emotions in check. "You didn't do a thing, Renata. I did."

"Now, hold on a minute," Deacon interrupted. "Normally I'd agree with you."

"She should have told you," Archer joined in. "She's in the wrong. Plain and simple."

Toben took heart in their support. And let his anger rise.

Deacon read the change in his posture and said, "But what you said yesterday was right—you've got to keep a cool head. If you're wanting to get close to this boy, you can't make an enemy out of his mother."

Toben nodded. He knew this. But, damn, he was angry. Furious. At her. And himself.

"I hate to pry here but—"

"I'm her son's father," Toben said, answering Renata's question before she could ask it. "Poppy White's boy? He's my son." Pride welled within him.

Renata's eyes went round. "Oh…well…" She blinked, the play of emotions on her face almost comical. "You… you didn't know?"

"She didn't tell him," Deacon offered.

Renata slumped back against the counter.

"Wrong. Plain and simple," Archer repeated, smacking his hat against his thigh. "Gotta get back to the refuge. Think before you act." He nodded at Toben, grabbed two pastries and headed back to his truck.

"I don't know what to say," Renata said. "Does Tandy know?"

Toben shook his head. He hadn't told his twin sister. He couldn't. She'd be just as devastated as he was—but for her own reasons. Besides, he didn't want everyone involved in his business. Having Archer, Deacon and Renata involved was three people too many in his book. "I'm trying to keep some kind of lid on it for now. Hard enough trying to figure things out on my own without getting the family involved."

"Guess that means I'm supposed to keep my mouth shut?" she asked. "Did you tell Archer that?"

Toben shook his head. "Figured he wouldn't say much, considering the topic."

Renata nodded. "Probably right. If it's not horses or Eden and the girls, he doesn't have much to say."

He glanced at the wall clock. "Daylight's a-wasting."

"If you've got something to do, I can get started without you," Deacon offered.

His first instinct was to go. He didn't know who Poppy had in her life or what role he played in Rowdy's. But if the man had been around for a while, then Toben couldn't let himself get all fired up about it—in front of Rowdy. "I'm not sure now's the right time for a visit," he admitted. "I don't want to press my luck or do something stupid in the process."

"I hate to agree with Archer, but...'think before you act' is pretty good advice." Renata hugged him again. "And congratulations. You might not be ready for it yet, but the family's going to welcome your boy with open arms."

She was right. The Boones believed in family. And Rowdy was family.

He and Deacon headed out shortly afterward, intent on repairing one of the windmills. A tornado had skirted the ranch a couple of weeks back and the strong winds had damaged two of the blades, throwing off the spin and affecting the entire mechanism. With drought concerns on the rise, the windmill needed to be working so the livestock had plenty of water.

By the time the sun was high, they'd replaced the two blades. They ate a late lunch in the mill's long shadow, barely a word said between them.

It took effort, but Toben kept all thoughts of Poppy at bay. Rowdy not so much. He wanted to do something with his son—but what? That was the question. How did he make up for six years in a couple of days? It would take time to earn the boy's trust—he knew that. But patience had never been one of his strengths. If he had it his way, he and Rowdy would jump right into it—father and son. Something he figured Poppy wasn't ready for.

He pushed aside her image, the lingering sound of her laughter as they'd sat on her porch enjoying pie. He loaded his toolbox into the back of the truck, frustrated all over again.

They headed to the vaccination shed next. Toben's uncle Teddy, owner of the entire ranch, had plans to vaccinate the cattle next week. It was no small undertaking, something that required working chutes, sturdy pens and all hands on deck. Safety was a top priority on the ranch—for the animals and the employees. A faulty chute or damaged pen could cause disaster. Between him and Deacon, they tested every fence, chute and gate latch that afternoon.

"I'm calling it," Deacon said, pouring water over the back of his head.

"Tired already?" Toben teased, smiling. They'd worked hard. Uncle Teddy would be happy.

"Damn straight," Deacon answered. "And hungry. Those were some sad sandwiches you packed."

Toben laughed. "I didn't hear you complain when you were eating them." He climbed in the truck as Deacon made the engine roar to life. He wiped his face with his bandanna and hung his arm out the window. He glanced at the dash. It was only six thirty-five. Not too late to stop by for a visit.

"You going over there?" Deacon asked.

"Thinking about it," he murmured. *All damn day.* He'd had a welcome-enough reception the night before. But now that another man was in Poppy's house, would that still be the case?

Chapter Five

A steady cloud of dust rose up behind the white truck pulling up her drive. It read Boone Ranch on the side—sending Poppy's stomach into knots and Rowdy running down the steps to meet the truck.

"He call?" Mitchell asked.

She shot Mitchell a look. "No, he didn't. But that doesn't mean you can't be polite and neighborly, Mitchell. Please."

He scowled. "Neighborly, Poppy? Him driving in here like he owns the place just feels like having dirt kicked in my face."

She shook her head, trying not to laugh at his over-the-top reaction. "No one's kicking dirt in anyone's face."

Mitchell's scowl didn't ease, so Poppy nudged him in the side. "Lighten up. No matter what, you hold a special place in Rowdy's heart. You know that."

His expression softened then, his attention shifting to her son. She never doubted Mitchell loved her boy. Mitchell's way with words and deep, resonant voice made him one of the most sought-after rodeo emcees—taking him out of the country a handful of times. But he always seemed to find time for them. In a way, Mitchell was Rowdy's father. A sobering realization when Rowdy's biological father was currently climbing out of the truck.

"You came!" Rowdy said. "I wanted you to meet Cheeto."

"He's here?" Toben asked.

"Mitchell brought him this morning. Man, was he glad to see me."

Rowdy laughed, and it warmed her through. She wasn't going to worry over why he was laughing. For now, she'd accept that Toben wanted to know their son. And be ready to ease Rowdy's loss when Toben moved on. The Toben Boone she'd known had been a restless soul. He was always talking about the next town, the next rodeo, the next prize…the next woman. He'd had no interest in planting roots or making commitments.

Maybe it was her? Maybe committing to her, to their son, was the reason he'd turned his back on her—on them both.

It's been seven years. People change.

But that sounded too good to be true.

"Evening," Toben said, tipping his hat.

"Toben," she said. "This is Mitchell Lee. Mitchell, Toben Boone. Well, you might know each other from the circuit?"

Toben's eyes tightened a little, his blue gaze bouncing back and forth between the two of them before he held out his hand. "The emcee? I remember you," Toben said, offering a tight smile.

"That's me," Mitchell agreed, his tone anything but welcoming. "I remember you, too."

She wasn't the only one who noticed. Everything about Toben stiffened. From his back to his jaw, he bristled. Poppy bit back her irritation. At least they shook hands, even if the tension between them was so thick it might just knock them both to the ground.

"Wanna meet him?" Rowdy asked, oblivious.

Toben and Mitchell were still sizing each other up, their mutual head-to-toe assessment almost comical. Almost.

"Sure he does," Poppy said, desperate to end the silent standoff. "Right, Toben? You want to meet Rowdy's horse?"

Toben's attention immediately shifted to Rowdy, his posture relaxing and his smile—that damn smile—returning. "Yes, sir. How'd he make the trip?"

"He's a good traveler," Rowdy said, kicking a rock. "We were always going somewhere. But not now." He smiled up at Toben. "We're here to stay."

Poppy felt that now-familiar unease settle in her stomach. They *had* been here to stay. Now she didn't know what the hell to do. She wanted a place Rowdy could grow up strong and happy, with good friends who watched him grow, helped him become a good man. She'd thought that Stonewall Crossing would be all those things and more.

"I'm glad to hear that," Toben said. "Did your mom tell you the Boones founded Stonewall Crossing?"

She heard Mitchell snort softly and stepped back, hard, on his toe with the heel of her boot. She didn't need him complicating a situation that was already far beyond her normal level of complication.

If Toben heard him, and it would be pretty hard to miss, he gave no indication. For that, Poppy was thankful. And confused. Everything about *this* Toben was confusing and frustrating.

"Really?" Rowdy asked.

Toben nodded. "This place is part of your family. When you come riding at the Boone Ranch, you'll get to meet a whole passel of aunts, uncles, great-uncles, cousins... You name it."

Rowdy's eyes were round. "You mean it's not just Dot and Otis?" The relief in his voice made the three adults laugh.

"How many kids do you have?" Mitchell asked.

The hard look Toben leveled the man's way made alarm

bells go off. "One," he answered, running a tentative hand over Rowdy's riotous curls.

The look of awe on Toben's face shook Poppy to the bone. The man Poppy had known wasn't capable of real emotion. He was a player. Life had been a series of games, challenges and conquests. He'd never been careful with his words…or his choice of women. He'd have punched Mitchell by now, or insulted him.

Seeing him standing here looking at Rowdy like he was his whole world wasn't something Poppy was prepared to handle. "Go on," she encouraged. "Dinner will be ready soon."

"Can he stay for dinner, Ma?" Rowdy asked. "Mitchell's grilling since the stove keeps catching fire."

"Not sure I got enough ribs, Rowdy." Mitchell's answer was quick.

Toben's jaw locked, but his attention stayed on Rowdy. "Better not. I like ribs. Might not be enough for you. Or Dot and Otis. Where are Dot and Otis?"

"Video game," she and Rowdy answered in unison.

Toben shook his head, staring out over the three hundred acres she'd just purchased for her family with an appreciative eye. Poppy nodded. She didn't get it either. When she'd been their age, she was climbing trees, skipping rocks and riding any animal she could climb onto.

"Let's go," Rowdy said, grabbing Toben's hand and pulling him toward the far pasture. Cheeto was there, waiting for Rowdy, his head resting on the fence line and his ears cocked forward.

Toben kept holding Rowdy's hand. And her son noticed. His happiness was all she wanted. Maybe…maybe Toben could be a part of that.

"He hasn't changed much." Mitchell's words snapped her out of it.

"What was that?" she asked. "I don't need you getting territorial, Mitchell. I need you to be my friend. I can't be worried about you and Toben throwing punches to establish the pecking order around here. I'm the one in charge, got it?"

Mitchell smiled down at her. He was tall, well over six feet. "I hear you, Pops. Don't get all riled up. I'll behave."

She crossed her arms over her chest, waiting.

"I'll try. I get that he has a right to know his son. You just promise me you won't let him worm his way back into your heart, and I'll leave it alone."

Poppy stared at Mitchell, horrified. "He was never in my heart—"

"Pops," Mitchell interrupted. "Come on, now. I was there, remember?"

She glared, then stomped past him and into the house. His heavy footsteps told her he was following. "I don't know where you come up with this stuff. I wasn't heartbroken over him. I was heartsick for my baby. There's a huge difference." She'd been lying so long there was no way she was going to change her story now.

"Pops." His tone was soothing.

"Don't Pops me. Get the grill started while I get this corn cooking. Hopefully, I won't burn down the damn house." She turned her back on him, refusing to let the concern in his gray eyes soften her anger.

"Fine, fine." Mitchell chuckled. "Wish I could skip the preseason exhibition tour. I don't like leaving y'all alone right now."

She spun on her heel then, outraged. "Mitchell Lee, we do just fine on our own, thank you. I love it when you visit. Rowdy loves it, too. But don't think, for one minute, that I can't manage my life without you."

Mitchell's smile grew. "Or any man."

"Or any man. I have no interest in raising two boys on my own," she added, snapping.

"That's all I needed to hear." Mitchell's smile was entirely too smug.

"See, I told you." Dot was leaning against the doorway, watching them. "They do act like it."

"Huh, guess so," Otis added.

"Act like what?" Mitchell asked.

"You're married," Dot answered. "You argue just like our parents. And you're always around."

"You gonna marry her?" Otis asked.

Mitchell smiled at Poppy, teasing her and loving every minute of it. "I've tried, but she won't have me."

Poppy burst out laughing then. He didn't want to marry a woman he thought of as his sister. "Okay, you two, since you're here, how about some help setting the table?"

The both groaned, and complained, and argued, but they did it.

"Where's Rowdy?" Dot asked.

"Yeah, why isn't he helping out?" Otis joined in, placing each fork on the table with a heavy thump.

"He's out with Cheeto. Horses need a lot of work." Poppy continued chopping salad, keeping a close watch on the ears of corn boiling on the stove. So far, the smoke was minimal.

"Mom won't let us have a pet," Otis said.

"Because you killed the fish," Dot explained.

"What happened?" Poppy turned, grabbing the chance to engage with her niece and nephew.

"We each picked out a betta fish. Mine was all pretty and pink and red," Dot said, folding napkins. "His was boy colored."

"I didn't know they wouldn't get along," Otis protested. "Who knew fish could do that?"

"That's why they come in separate cups, Otis. They

need their own personal space." Dot shook her head. "His fish killed my fish and then he was so freaked out he gave his away."

"Oh." Poppy frowned. "Poor little fish."

"And that's why we can't have a pet." Dot shook her head. "It's your fault, so stop whining about it."

And just like that, Otis snapped. "Shut up, Dot! I'm sick of you being so bossy."

Dot's smile was hard. "Because you know I'm right?"

"Hold on." Poppy stepped forward.

"You're a brat." Otis's voice shook.

"You're a baby," Dot bit back. "A crybaby."

The color bleached from Otis's cheeks before he flushed red.

"Guys, enough." Poppy tried to reprimand them—at the same time the burner caught fire on the stove and the smoke alarm screamed to life. "Dammit!"

She heard her niece and nephew in the background, heard the clatter of cutlery on the wood-planked floor, but couldn't do much until she'd located the fire extinguisher and put out the fire. She spun, horrified to see Dot punch Otis in the arm—hard—and Otis push Dot.

"Stop, right now." She stepped between them. "I don't ever, ever, want to see the two of you get physical with one another. I don't care how mad you are at each other. You have no right to raise a hand to someone else. Do you understand me?"

Dot opened her mouth.

"She started it," Otis argued.

"Doesn't matter." Poppy sighed. "No matter who started it. Talk, argue, scream if you have to. There's a right and a wrong way to argue. Getting physical is wrong. Okay?" She was suddenly aware of Toben and Rowdy standing in the door to the kitchen.

Toben was watching her, his blue eyes unwavering—and far too intense for her liking.

Poppy tore her gaze from his and placed a hand on Otis's and Dot's shoulders, squeezing. "You two are just like me and your mother. In time, you'll realize how lucky you are to have each other—become trusted friends." She and Rose had been that way. They'd been each other's biggest fans, building each other up. Until Poppy got pregnant. Her pregnancy had forever changed their dynamic. "You need to have each other's backs, not go for each other's jugulars."

"What's a jugular?" Rowdy asked.

"She means throat," Toben clarified.

"Oh, right." Rowdy nodded. "That makes sense."

"Ribs are ready." Mitchell entered, carrying a tray stacked high with food.

She frowned, knowing damn well there was enough food for Toben to join them. "No corn tonight." She pointed at the stovetop covered in white foam. "Salad."

"And leftover pie," Rowdy offered. "Sure you can't stay?"

Toben eyed the mountain of ribs and shook his head. "Not tonight."

"Maybe you can come grill. Mitchell's the best at it—no offense, Mom—but he's leaving soon for work." Rowdy was offering up far too much information. "Where are you going again, Mitchell?"

She heard the tightness in Mitchell's throat as he said, "Montana, then Wyoming."

"I'll be here." Toben smiled. "If that's all right with you, Poppy?"

Poppy couldn't resist the eagerness on her son's face. In two days, Mitchell would be gone and she'd have to face Toben alone. His smile, his eyes, his far-too-tempting body... A body that seemed to ignite something molten deep inside her. She needed to get a handle on that, and fast. If Toben was going to be part of Rowdy's life, that was one thing. But inviting Toben back into *her* life was a mistake she couldn't afford to make.

A THOROUGH INSPECTION of Poppy's barn had revealed some wood rot on two of the stalls. Whenever Toben came upon some wood scraps or hardware he thought were useful, he'd throw it in the back of the truck. Why he felt compelled to fix her barn, he didn't know. It was her place, a damn fine place at that. And knowing her, he was sure she'd want to keep it that way. So…he wanted to help.

For Rowdy.

Keeping Poppy happy kept Rowdy happy.

Or at least, that was what he told himself.

The only thing he was dreading was the conversation he needed to have with his twin sister, Tandy. She'd never been a fan of Poppy White. In her mind, Poppy was the one who broke Toben's heart and put him on the path to destruction. But then, his twin didn't know he'd been the one who did the actual leaving. Maybe she was right. Maybe loving—and losing—Poppy had been the tipping point.

It didn't matter now. Best to leave the past in the past—for the future's sake.

He found her at the vet hospital, viewing blood samples through a microscope. "Hey, sis, what's up?"

"Um, I'm in shock. What brings you here?" She slid off her stool and hugged him. "You'd think I'd see more of you since we're in the same town. Other than the monthly get-together, that is."

Toben frowned, staring at the floor. "Yeah, well, I'm sorry about that. I get busy."

"I know. I hear all about it," Tandy returned, shooting him a disapproving look.

He grinned. Some of his favorite late-night sports included veterinary students. "Never heard any complaints."

"You wouldn't." She sighed. "Makes it hard to hear a damn thing when the only thing exchanged is sex."

"Let's leave my recreational activities for another time, okay?" Toben shook his head. "Have time for lunch?"

She glanced at the clock on the wall. "Is it really one already? Sure."

The vet hospital was on the other side of the highway, a world away from everything that made Stonewall Crossing a visit to times past. Here the buildings were new and eco-friendly, with solar panels on the roofs, fast-food eating establishments and several apartment complexes for the students of University of East Texas.

They picked one of the burger joints, found a small booth and placed their order before Tandy finally asked, "So what's the crisis?" She spun her sweet tea with her straw.

"Crisis?" he echoed. Poppy reappearing in his life was... odd. But Rowdy? He didn't classify any of this as a crisis. "I have something to tell you."

Tandy nodded. "So tell me."

He sat back, glancing around the restaurant, drawing his courage.

"Just spit it out, Toben." Tandy was all smiles. "We can figure it out."

"Okay." Toben blew out a slow breath. "You remember Poppy White?"

Her smile disappeared and she leaned back against her seat. "Of course I do."

"She moved to Stonewall Crossing—"

"So you're leaving?" Tandy frowned. "Dammit, Toben, you're finally putting down some roots. Don't let her chase you off. Please. I know Uncle Teddy, Hunter—hell, even

Archer—need you on the ranch." She sat forward. "And me. I'd like you to stick around."

"I'm not leaving. Turns out we... She has a kid. And he's mine." His words were soft.

Tandy's expression shifted, from anger to nothing. He knew that expression, blank and stiff and hiding so much pain. And it killed him to see it. "What?" she whispered.

"His name is Rowdy."

She stared at him, not saying a word.

"Tandy?" He reached for her, taking his hand in hers.

She blinked.

"She says she tried to reach me."

"You believe her?" she asked.

He sat back, running a hand over the back of his neck. He'd been thinking about that very thing. A lot. After he left her, he'd gone a little crazy. He'd finally got what he wanted: Poppy in his bed. But the morning after, everything was...different. Hell, he'd felt different. He'd held her close, soft and warm against him, watching her sleep. And his damn heart had felt as if it were on the verge of pounding itself out of his chest. He'd been a damn fool to think Poppy was just another good time. She'd been... they'd been...real. Too real for someone like him. He'd only mess things up, hurting them both along the way. So he'd grabbed his boots and run, but he'd never found an escape.

After Poppy, everything *had* been different. It had been awful. No matter how many soft and sweet women he took back to his room, he'd wish it were Poppy he was holding. Hundreds of miles, countless six-packs of beer and far too many bottles of whiskey later, he'd done his best to let her go. He didn't remember much clearly. It was all sort of blurred and horrible. Made worse when her letters started coming. Letters he'd shredded without opening, too chicken to face words she'd written. Or what those words might do to him. She *had* tried. Over and over.

It was his fault. All of it. It wasn't easy to accept. "I...I do."

"What does she want?" she asked. "What's she after, showing up now?"

"She didn't know I was here. She bought the old Travis place—off Highway One-Twenty-One? Plans on settling down, raise Rowdy here and opening a shop on Main Street." He smiled.

"Rowdy?" Tandy nodded. "Sounds like you. Strange how things turn out."

"Strange, yes. But it's given me a second chance." He rubbed his neck again. "I don't want to screw this up."

Tandy sighed, her posture easing. "Then you need to make things right, Toben." Her words were raw. "We know what it's like to grow up without a father, how it eats at you, makes you doubt your worth. Give your son better than that." She paused, her voice going hard. "Be there. Stay."

He heard the pain in her voice. "That's the plan."

"Well...good." She leaned back so the waitress could put her salad in front of her. "What about Poppy?"

"She hasn't changed." He tried to keep his voice neutral.

"You're okay with that?" she asked.

He shot her a look. "I'm not some lovesick kid, Tandy. Life goes on."

"This is me," she pointed out. "So knock off the manly thing. She mattered, a lot. I don't know what she did to you, but I remember how you fell apart. I don't want you to go through that."

She hadn't done a damn thing. Not that it mattered now. "She's off the market and, no matter what you think, I won't steal another man's woman." He took a bite of his hamburger.

"That's nice to hear." Tandy grinned, pushing her salad around but not taking a bite.

"Talk about a high opinion." He laughed.

"I love you, even when I don't understand why you do what you do—which is the majority of the time. Maybe having someone watching you, someone that matters, will help you…grow up and be the man I know you can be." She shook her head. "And don't get offended—you know I'm right."

Toben swallowed, shrugging off the flare of irritation that her brutally honest words stirred. In the few days since Rowdy had entered his life, he'd been more intentional with his words and actions. "Doesn't mean I want to hear it…" He glanced at her. "Thing is, I don't know how to do that. To be a father a son can be proud of. But I want to."

"Oh, Toben." Tandy set her fork down and leaned forward. "You do. Think of everything you wished we had—everything that would have mattered. That's what you do for him."

Toben nodded.

"Can I meet him?" she asked.

He smiled. "Of course. I'm just biding my time until Mitchell leaves town."

Tandy's brow arched. "Why? If this guy is a fixture in their lives, shouldn't you come to terms with that?"

Toben focused on his food then. "I'm doing the best I can. Right now Rowdy comes first. It was clear Poppy's boyfriend wasn't a fan of me. I don't see the point in making things harder by being where I'm not wanted."

Tandy sighed. "And Poppy's take?"

"We haven't had much time to talk." He took another bite of his burger. It didn't help that every time they were together, talking was the last thing on his mind. She unleashed a sort of charge along his skin, heightening his awareness and drawing him in. If he had something important to say, one look from her chocolate-brown eyes erased it from his mind. And made him itch to touch her.

"Don't you think you should make time?" Tandy brought him back to reality. "If you're going to raise Rowdy together, setting ground rules is a good place to start."

The thought of sitting down with Poppy, laying out a plan for raising Rowdy... He could just see the flash of temper in her eyes. "Guess so," he admitted grudgingly. "It's not too soon?"

"Too soon? I'm surprised you're sitting here. I'd be there, dogging his every step and learning everything I can about him." She shook her head, her expression shifting again. "Oh... You're worried about making her angry?"

He nodded. "I might believe her, about trying to tell me. But I don't know if she believes me that I didn't know."

She stared at him for a long time.

"What?" he asked, setting the remains of his burger on the plate.

"Put yourself in her shoes. I guess I'd be hard-pressed to believe you, too." Tandy shrugged, taking a bite of her salad.

He steered the conversation into more neutral territory. She was working as a vet technician in the teaching hospital but hoped to get accepted into the veterinary medicine program that fall. She'd made the waiting list...and the waiting was taking its toll. He, on the other hand, had every confidence she'd be accepted. She was the smart one; she worked hard. Considering how hard the last few years had been on her, losing the man she loved and the baby they were expecting, it was about time something good came her way.

He dropped her off at the veterinary hospital and crossed over the highway, driving down Main Street. Poppy's big red truck was parked in front of her shop. The lead-glass door was propped open—so Toben took it as an invitation.

He pulled in next to her truck, turned off the ignition and climbed out. "Poppy?" he called from the doorway.

He wandered inside, running his hands along the woodwork of the shelves. The store hadn't looked this good in years, all detailed craftsmanship, quirky cubbies and custom built-ins. He heard the telltale sound of a grinder in the back room and headed that way, pausing when he came to a stack of rodeo memorabilia.

Pictures, newspaper clippings, certificates, plaques, ribbons... Poppy's career. An impressive career, one she should be proud of. One their son was proud of.

He flipped through the framed pictures, pausing at a picture of Poppy and Rowdy sitting on their mounts. Rowdy was little—his hat on his head, tiny hands gripping the saddle horn.

"Can I help you?" Mitchell Lee stood in the doorway, wearing an openly hostile expression and holding a shelf.

Toben refused to be goaded. "I was looking for Poppy."

"She's home with the kids." Mitchell placed the shelf against the wall and wiped his hands on a bandanna. "Need something?"

He shook his head. "Saw her truck and thought I'd stop by, see if I could help."

Mitchell tucked the bandanna into his back pocket. "Why?"

"Why what?"

"Why do you want to help?" Mitchell asked. "I know you're hoping to connect with Rowdy but helping Poppy doesn't connect you with your son."

Toben waited, sensing Mitchell had more to say on the matter. Not that he necessarily wanted to hear what this man had to say.

"Poppy says you didn't know anything about Rowdy? That this was all some sort of surprise?" The corner of Mitchell's mouth cocked up, a challenge in his eyes. "Thing is, I don't buy that. And...I don't like you."

Toben's laugh was pure surprise.

"More important, I don't like what you're trying to do." Mitchell put his hands on his hips, his eyes narrowing.

"And what am I trying to do?"

"Get even." Mitchell's voice was sharp.

Toben's heart stopped.

"She hurt you. You want to hurt her." Mitchell stepped forward. "I'd advise against it. No way I'm going to let you hurt either one of them."

He wasn't laughing anymore. He didn't want to hurt Rowdy. Or Poppy—even if he was still pissed at the circumstances. "You don't know me." His fists clenched at his sides.

"I know of you. And what I know is enough." Mitchell shook his head. "Poppy and Rowdy are *my* family and you're not going to change that. Consider this a warning." He stepped closer. "You mess with the bull, you'll get the horns."

Toben clenched his jaw, holding himself rigid. He wouldn't take the bait. He wouldn't knock that smug smile off Mitchell's face—even if his hand itched to do so.

"Course, your rodeo record shows you were shit with the bulls. Your best sport was charming the jeans off every buckle bunny that crossed your path. Poppy—and Rowdy—deserve better than that."

Toben didn't have time to think. His fist flew out, connecting with Mitchell's set jaw and rattling the bones of his hand. "Dammit," he muttered. He'd knocked Mitchell back but not down.

The man straightened—a scowl on his face. "You sure you want to do this?"

Toben didn't have time to answer. Mitchell's fist slammed into his left eye. For a split second, all Toben saw was stars and blackness. A sharp throb, a blinding heat... He shook his head.

"Much as I'd like to finish this, Rowdy wouldn't approve," Mitchell snapped.

Toben flexed his hands, the fight going out of him. He'd just done what he'd sworn not to do—lose his cool. He stared at the ceiling, blinking until his vision cleared. "I don't need to prove anything to you—"

"You just did. You want to raise a hotheaded boy? Someone who throws a fist before thinking things through? I knew what I was doing. And that you'd swing." He shook his head, rubbing his jaw. "You've got a hell of a lot to prove to Rowdy. And Poppy..." He shook his head. "You don't get it. You don't get hard work or sacrifice... Poppy's been taking hits for years and never complained. Nothing stopped her. She never gave up. After Rowdy's birth, after the accident, after losing her grandfather—she got up every damn time. She's a fighter."

Toben stared at the man, shaken by the desperation in Mitchell's voice. Toben understood. Mitchell Lee loved Poppy and Toben was a threat. He felt a grudging respect for the man. Poppy had every right to someone who'd love and protect her so fiercely. And though it was none of Toben's business, he couldn't help but wonder if Poppy loved Mitchell, too.

Chapter Six

"You got everything?" Poppy asked, shifting the inner tube to her other arm.

"How long will this take?" Dot asked.

"Why are we doing this?" Otis whined.

"It's hot," Rowdy said. "And it's fun."

"Can you swim?" Otis countered.

Rowdy nodded, smiling at Poppy. "Come on, Ma." He ran ahead, following the dirt path that cut down and around behind their small house to the river below.

Poppy paused, appreciating what was now her property. There was a slight hill leading to the river, several tall oak and pecan trees casting patches of cover. She could only imagine how the place would look when the bluebonnets were blooming. Her gaze wandered, imagining a sea of blue, waving in the breeze.

At the base of the hill, the Medina River waited. The shore of the river was made of pebbles and rock. Small fish, more rocks and bright green patches of green moss were visible beneath the clear water. She'd read enough on the area to know that its depth varied widely, so she didn't want the kids exploring on their own—not yet.

Rowdy walked out onto one especially large flat rock that extended into the river.

"How deep is it?" Otis asked.

"Not deep," Rowdy answered. "I can see the bottom."

"Wait for me," Poppy called out.

"Going tubing?" Toben's voice at her side made her jump. "Sorry."

"I didn't hear you." She turned, instantly aware of the crackle in the air between them. Suddenly her cutoff jeans and pink tank top seemed revealing—her bikini underneath downright indecent. Not that there was anything wrong with what she was wearing. He'd seen her in a lot less. Besides, everything she owned was modest. And they were going tubing, after all. But she didn't miss the way he looked at her, those blue eyes...

"Your face?" she asked, angry colors marring his cheek and brow, reaching up. She hadn't meant to touch him, to feel how soft the hair at his temple was or note the slight hitch in his breath.

His hand encircled her wrist. "Nothing worth talking about." His voice was gruff and deep, making her toes curl against the rubber soles of her flip-flops.

His hold was gentle, the roughened skin of his thumb brushing slowly against the inside of her wrist. The summer breeze blew, making his curls brush her fingertips and his scent flood her nostrils. Why did it have to be this way between them? Fragments of memory, the jolt of sensation. How could she still remember how he tasted? How it felt to be pressed beneath him? An instantaneous ache racked her. She pulled her hand back, ignoring the tingles—ignoring the white-hot want.

Worse, he seemed just as affected as she was. His gaze centered on her lips, the muscles of his jaw clenching tightly.

She shifted the inner tube, holding it in front of her, needing a barrier. "It's a hot day. Figured we could swim a little."

He nodded, his gaze sweeping over her face.

"You coming?" Rowdy called. When he turned and saw Toben, his smile grew. "Hi! You coming, too?"

Poppy held her breath. On the one hand, it was a bad idea. On the other, she wouldn't mind the help. Did Otis and Dot swim well? She'd asked and they'd leveled their signature dismissive look her way—she had no idea what that was supposed to mean.

"Okay with you?" he asked.

She nodded, unable to look him in the eye.

"Give me a sec," he yelled, running back toward the house.

"Stupid, stupid, stupid," she muttered all the way down to the river. "No, Toben, you can't come with us," she whispered. "Maybe next time. Maybe never."

"What'd you say, Ma?" Rowdy asked, sticking his feet in the river. "Ah man, it's cold."

"Is it?" she asked.

Rowdy nodded, splashing her.

She squealed, shielding her face and giggling. "Rowdy!"

She wriggled out of her shorts and top, kicked off her flip-flops and eased into the cold, clear water with a sigh. "This is perfect."

The kids waded into the water with her, laughing and splashing each other until they were all dripping wet. Seeing them having fun, acting like kids, made the day that much sweeter.

"How long can you hold your breath?" Dot asked, disappearing below the water.

While the kids took turns, Poppy did her best not to keep checking the path. He'd get here when he got here—no point in rushing things. But the longer he took, the more anxious she grew. Finally, he was heading down the hill—and she groaned, ducking under the water. She should have told him no, should have made him leave. She let the water's icy temperature cool her down. When she resurfaced, she focused all her energy on keeping a blank face.

Considering what a fine male specimen Toben Boone was, that took a lot of focus.

Toben's cutoff jeans were uneven, but the length of muscled legs revealed was impressive. He wore a short-sleeved button-down shirt…hanging open to reveal far too much of him. His jeans rested low on his hips. The sharp cut and dip of muscles of his chest and stomach had her dipping beneath the water again.

When she came up, Toben was laughing.

"Did you hear that, Ma?" Rowdy asked.

She shook her head. "What?"

"Otis's joke," Rowdy said.

Otis had told a joke? She glanced at her nephew. He was smiling. So was Dot. Were they really having a good time? She grinned. "What joke?"

"What do you call a bear with no teeth?" Otis asked.

Poppy shrugged.

"A gummy bear," Otis answered.

She laughed.

"Next time the water's up, we could float down to the first bridge," Toben said. "Not much current right now, but it sure feels good."

"Your eye's all messed up." Dot pointed out. "Looks like it hurts."

He nodded. "It doesn't feel good."

"What happened?" Otis asked.

Toben glanced at her. "I walked into something."

Poppy frowned. The thing he'd walked into was sporting an angry bruise on his jaw. Mitchell had left before Rowdy woke up, claiming he had an early flight to Reno. Poppy suspected he'd left before sunup because he didn't want to upset her son. She knew boys would be boys, but why would Mitchell and Toben exchange blows? What good would that do? Maybe Toben hadn't changed. The Toben she remembered had either been picking up women or picking fights.

"Next time you should watch where you're going," Rowdy said, swimming to the flat rock.

Toben was still looking at her. "There won't be a next time."

She hoped that meant he and Mitchell had reached an understanding. If she was going to do this, raise Rowdy together with Toben, no one should be throwing punches.

"I'm jumping," Rowdy said, leaping off the rock.

The water splashed, eliciting laughter all around.

Poppy smiled, watching them together. For the first time in days, the three kids were getting along.

"How deep does it get?" Otis asked.

"I'll find out." Poppy swam out. The water they'd been swimming in wasn't deep. She could sit and the water reached her chin. But in the middle of the river, she had to stand on tiptoe in places. "Too deep."

Surprisingly, none of them argued. They took turns jumping off the rock, splashing each other and spinning in the inner tube she'd carried down.

Toben surfaced beside her. "Good to see them smiling. I was beginning to think they didn't have it in them."

Poppy nodded, acutely aware of how close he was. "What happened with Mitchell?" she asked.

He swam around her, putting them face-to-face. "Does it matter?"

Her gaze locked with his. "Yes."

"He the one you're engaged to?" he asked, his voice wavering slightly.

"No." She opened her mouth, then closed it. "Does it matter?"

His blue eyes narrowed but he didn't say anything. Instead he disappeared beneath the water. Seconds later his hand grabbed her ankle and he tugged her under.

Poppy plunged beneath the water, swallowed in sensation. His hands sliding up her bare stomach. His arm sliding around her waist, anchoring her against him. He was warm and strong, his bare chest pressing against hers and lighting a fire inside her. She was going to drown in this—not the water. And then he was tugging her back to the surface.

"He got you, Ma," Rowdy said, laughing.

She sputtered, her hands gripping Toben's shoulders until there was air in her lungs. But seeing his chest, the rounded muscles of his shoulders, his thick neck and square jaw... She was gasping for air. Her fingers curled into the wet fabric of his shirt.

Don't look at him. Don't do it.

Her eyes met his. And the hunger she saw there, raw and fierce, had her pushing off his chest and under the water. She swam back to the rock, pulling herself out and onto the flat surface. It was hot, so she spread her shirt out and sat, dazed.

"Don't leave, Ma," Rowdy called out, splashing her with water.

"I'm not going anywhere," she answered, waving at him. "Just needed a...drink." She stretched, tugging her insulated lunchbag to her side and pulling a water bottle out. Her hands shook as she opened the bottle and took a sip.

Toben was tossing the kids into the water, their laughter and pleas for more assuring her that he wasn't affected. He'd dunked her in river water and she was having a visceral reaction. One that had her throbbing. The look in his eyes... She blew out an unsteady breath. Maybe she was wrong. Maybe she was seeing what she wanted to see.

She wrung the water from her hair, angry. That was not

what she wanted to see. She had no interest in reliving her disastrous affair with Toben. Even if she had enjoyed every second of it at the time...

No, certainly not. She had big plans. Her shop, being an involved mom, living a normal life... Toben Boone didn't fit that mold. If he wanted to be a part of Rowdy's life, great. But she needed to let him know she wasn't part of that arrangement. And when she wasn't a mess, she'd tell him so.

She lay back, letting the hot sun warm her skin until her tension melted away.

"You'll get burned." Toben's voice was low.

She rolled over, refusing to look at him.

"Poppy, I'd like to introduce Rowdy to my family. We try to get together, the whole crew, once a month if we can. I thought I could show him the ranch, let him meet one or two people first? So the family gathering's not too overwhelming."

She pressed her eyes shut. Toben's family. Rowdy's family. For Poppy, family meant her son. Yes, she had her sister, but Rose had Bob and the kids and little time for anything else. She wouldn't begrudge her son more people to love him. She sat up, watching the kids still splashing in the river. "Okay."

Toben sat beside her, stretching his long legs out in front of him and crossing them at the ankles.

She leaned away, resting on one arm. Proximity seemed to have a direct impact on both of them.

"I brought some steaks to grill," he said. "Picked up some potato salad and a watermelon, too."

She glanced at him, surprised. He was, without a doubt, the most attractive man she'd ever seen. Every inch of him was rock hard and golden. His shirt was gone, his hair damp and his smile... She swallowed.

"I said I'd cook dinner," he explained, smiling at her.

She was mesmerized by the drop of water running onto Toben's well-muscled chest. She shivered, pulling her knees up and wrapping her arms around them. She hugged tight, resting her chin on her knees.

"So, Mitchell?" he asked, his voice gruff.

"Is a good man." Which was true. "He's important to Rowdy. And to me."

"I know."

His simple answer drew her attention back to him. But when his blue eyes searched hers, she turned back to the kids, who seemed completely oblivious to the charged energy pulsing around them.

"But if he's enough, why are you looking at me like that?"

"Ma," Rowdy called out. "Dot doesn't know how to float."

Poppy slid off the rock and into the water, eager for any distraction. "I can help with that."

"THAT WAS GREAT," Otis said, clearing his plate. "Thanks for the steak."

"And the watermelon," Dot added.

"You're welcome." Toben stood to clear the table.

"You cooked—I'll clean," Poppy said, pushing him back into the chair with a hand on his shoulder.

He wanted to cover her hand with his. He wanted to touch her. He flexed his hand and grabbed his tea, taking a long sip.

"When are we going riding?" Rowdy asked.

"Whenever you want." Toben was eager to see his boy in the saddle.

"How about tomorrow?"

Poppy stopped scrubbing long enough to say, "It's Monday, Rowdy, a workday."

"That mean you'll be too tired?" Rowdy asked. "Or have plans?"

Toben shook his head. "The only plans I have in the near future are the ones we make together." He wanted his son to know that he came first. As of now, Rowdy would always come first.

Rowdy's smile was answer enough.

Poppy's scrubbing started up again, more vigorous than before.

"How do you feel about coming out to the ranch?" he asked his son.

"Sure," Rowdy said, yawning.

"Can I call Mom?" Dot asked.

"Of course," Poppy said, turning off the water.

Dot and Otis hurried down the hallway.

"It's almost bedtime, though, so don't—"

But the guest room door closed, so Poppy didn't bother finishing her sentence.

"Ma." Rowdy stood, sliding his arm around her waist and pressing his head against her. "You're never gonna get sick, are you?"

Toben's heart lodged in his throat. He watched Poppy drop to her knees, hugging Rowdy close. "No, sir. You are stuck with me."

Rowdy's arms tightened around her. "Good. I like being stuck with you."

She laughed, gripping his shoulders. "Glad to hear it. Hit the shower."

Rowdy nodded, hugged her again and faced him. "I don't know what to call you."

Toben glanced at Poppy, taking in her fearful expression. "You can call me Toben." He cleared his throat, then swallowed. "Or you can call me Dad."

Rowdy nodded, his expression thoughtful.

"You don't have to decide right away," Poppy offered up.

"I've got to call him something," Rowdy argued. "I'll think on it. Okay?"

"Okay," Toben agreed.

He wasn't prepared for Rowdy's hug. But the boy gave strong, solid ones. Toben was gripped with a love so fierce he held on. His son's sweet smell, his small hands pressing against Toben's shoulders... This was his boy. And his boy was giving him this hug.

"'Night," Rowdy said, shooting him a devastating smile before hurrying from the kitchen. Toben stared after him, grappling with the longing that smile stirred. He didn't know what this was, how something so simple could impact him so severely, but Rowdy seemed to have turned everything on its ear.

A thump sounded behind him. But when he turned, the kitchen was empty. He pushed through the screen door and onto the porch. Poppy stood, hugging herself, at the far side of the porch—staring into the night sky.

Fireflies blinked, crickets chirped, and the distant snort and stomp of the horses was a familiar soundtrack. He and Tandy had been born in Montana, raised by his mother and aunts, but he'd never truly felt at home until he found his way to Texas. And this place, with his boy, felt the way he'd always imagined a real home would feel.

"He's falling hard for you." Poppy's voice was so soft he moved closer.

"That's good." He paused. "Isn't it?"

She turned to face him, tears shining in her eyes. "I want to believe in you, Toben. For Rowdy's sake. I want to believe that you're going to stay—to be a real father."

"What's stopping you?" He frowned.

"Are you serious?" she managed, sniffing angrily. "We have a history. I know you—"

"No, you don't. There's no history between *us*. I…I left before that could happen." He hated the vulnerability in his voice. But, dammit, it hurt. What was lost, what he'd taken from them all.

Her eyes went round. "Toben…this is about him. Every second of every day is about him." She pointed at the door. "He's put you on a pedestal his whole life. He—"

"Thank you," Toben interrupted.

She sputtered to a stop.

"I mean it. You could have trashed me—told him I didn't want him. But you didn't. And for that I am truly grateful." He paused, taking in every detail of her face. Her brown eyes were rimmed with gold. A perfectly round mole graced her upper left cheekbone. The middle of her full lower lip was flat—and tempting. So damn tempting. "You've done a good job."

"He's a good boy," she murmured, eyeing him warily.

He held his hands up. "I'm complimenting you. No strings."

Her eyes narrowed, darting to his mouth. "None?" The word was unsteady.

He felt a rush of desire, so hot and fast he gripped the porch railing. "What do you want me to say, Poppy?"

She shook her head, stepping back. "That you're here for Rowdy."

He stepped closer. "Nothing else?"

"No. Nothing else," she whispered, her brow furrowing. "Rowdy's all that matters. I don't have room for anything else."

"Not even Mitchell?" He couldn't keep the bite out of his voice.

She shook her head. "What do you have against him?"

Toben gripped the railing, fighting all the pent-up emotion that had been boiling inside him since Poppy told him the truth. He cleared his throat, swallowed...cleared his throat again. But he couldn't stop the words from spilling out. "He took my place. He had the time I should have had. He's had my son, my family, you... I should be the one taking care of Rowdy, defending your honor, making our son laugh and watching him grow." He swallowed, his temper warring with the bone-deep grief he felt. "And you let him." He sucked in a deep breath, the air stinging his empty lungs. "You let him." He stared at her, knowing there was nothing she could do or say to make this better—but hoping.

Her breathing accelerated, her eyes shadowed in the porch light, but she didn't say a thing. She looked angry... and sad. "It wasn't my first choice, him standing in. But... he was there when no one else was." Her voice shook. "No one."

What could he say to that? Poppy had always been so damn...independent. Thinking of her alone, needing someone, was hard to imagine. "I didn't know."

She nodded slowly. "Neither did I."

"That's supposed to make this okay?"

"No. Nothing can make this okay. Nothing can change what happened. I lived it. Alone." She stared at the door, her voice dropping. "I woke up and you were gone. I'd expected that. But then Rowdy came along and I...I..." She shook her head. "Every day I woke up, looked at my boy and knew you'd chosen not to be a part of his life."

Her words sliced through him, razor-sharp and enraging. "I. Didn't. Know," he ground out.

"You said that. But I tried to reach you. I left messages with everyone that answered your phone." She smiled, a hard, bitter smile. "And I wrote letters, sent some pictures." She shook her head. "When I didn't hear from you, what else was I supposed to think?"

Toben stared out into the night sky, grappling with her

words and the overwhelming waves of conflicted emotions crashing into him—again and again. He didn't remember much about that time. He was too caught up in missing her, too full of pride to hunt her down and too stubborn to let anyone know what he was going through. He'd been a fool. Considering he hadn't changed much, he was still a fool.

That reality stuck in his throat. He didn't want to be that man. He wanted to be…better.

He knew, staring at her, his chest heavy and his lungs hungry for air, he'd go back in time if he could. Her words filled him with shame. He didn't want to feel sorry for her. He didn't want to look at her and need to hold her close. He didn't want to wonder what would have happened if she'd woken up with him at her side—if he hadn't left her in that bed alone.

"It's late." She ran her hands down her thighs, anxious.

He didn't move, didn't know where to go from here. "I'll come get you all around six tomorrow?" He wanted Rowdy to see Boone Ranch and meet some of his family. He didn't want to rush things, he and Rowdy were just getting started. They had time now.

Poppy shook her head, crossing the porch. "Rowdy will be ready. No point in the rest of us going. See you then." She didn't look back as she pulled the front door closed behind her.

He stood on the porch, staring at her door, wishing things weren't so damn difficult. He crossed the yard, catching sight of the wood he'd brought to repair her stalls. "No point in leaving," he murmured as he climbed into the truck and headed to Poppy's barn.

Chapter Seven

Poppy held the tie of her rope, shaking all the kinks out of the large loop. She glanced at the kids, all watching her from the porch, and eyed her target. The barrel sat in the middle of the yard, offering her no resistance and no challenge. But if she was going to teach them how to throw a lariat with any confidence, they needed to start small.

Her right hand fed the rope up, coiling it into her left hand until the length was neatly wound and ready for use. She fed a little length into her loop and swung the circle, quick right-to-left spins, before aiming. The rope flew and settled around the barrel with ease.

Three voices cheered from the porch, making her smile and bow. "Who wants to try it?"

The three of them looked at one another.

"Nope," Dot said, stepping back.

"I'll try," Otis said, hesitating before walking to her side.

He was quick, picking up the basics and figuring out how to get the best precision with his hold.

"Looks like you've got a little rodeo in you." She patted Otis's shoulder when he lassoed the barrel for the third time in a row.

"Rowdy can have a turn now," Otis said, clearly pleased with himself.

But Rowdy was staring down the road.

Poppy glanced at her watch. It was almost seven and no Toben. No phone call either. She hoped he had a hell of a good reason for disappointing Rowdy. One that didn't include drinking, a fight or a woman.

Rowdy tried, but his heart wasn't in it. He was distracted and irritable. By the time the sun was dropping, Poppy resorted to drastic actions.

"Who wants ice cream?" she asked. "Let's head into town, to the café."

"Can I get a milk shake?" Dot asked.

"Sure," Poppy agreed, hurrying them into her truck.

"What if he shows up while we're gone?" Rowdy asked.

"I'm sure he'll call before he makes the drive," she answered.

"Think he's okay?"

She nodded stiffly. If he was okay, Poppy would make damn sure he knew that what he'd done tonight was *not* okay. Loudly. With lots of curse words. Rowdy had been looking forward to riding Boone Ranch and spending time with Toben.

She took her time on the winding roads. The kids chattered away about what sort of ice cream they wanted, how good Otis was at throwing a rope and how they wanted to go swimming again tomorrow.

"I can't believe we're going home soon," Dot said, sighing. "Feels like we've been with you forever."

Poppy laughed. She wasn't going to argue with her niece. It hadn't been an easy visit, but she was glad things were less painful. Rose and Bob would arrive Sunday evening, stay a few days and leave with the kids Tuesday night. "It's been fun. And ice cream will make it better."

The one café on Main Street was crowded, so she and the kids took seats at the counter.

Poppy ordered a small vanilla milk shake, shaking her

head at the orders the kids placed. Whatever—it was a treat. And Rowdy's grin was back.

She glanced around the café, smiling and nodding at those she made eye contact with. Loneliness gripped her. Maybe it was the old couple sharing a sundae in the corner or the teens making out in a booth, but there were times Poppy wanted that sort of connection. Mitchell was as close as she'd come. Not in the passionate, make-out-in-the-corner sort of way. Kissing, intimacy, had been awkward and forced between them—not the way it was meant to be. Unlike her experience with Toben. That night had been all passion, white-hot, plucking every nerve ending and leaving her aching.

"Like it?" Rowdy asked, glancing doubtfully at her shake.

"Want a sip?" she asked, offering him the straw.

He shook his head. "Want a bite?"

She assessed the pile of brownies, ice cream, whipped cream, sprinkles and a cherry on top. "I'm not sure what to eat."

Rowdy scooped off a healthy spoonful of ice cream, far too big to fit into her mouth, and offered her the spoon. He grinned, waiting for her reaction. Poppy opened her mouth as wide as she could, knowing whipped cream smeared her chin and the tip of her nose and not caring in the least.

Until Toben arrived, his shirt rumpled and his jeans covered in dirt and grease. He took one look at her puffed out cheeks and burst out laughing.

She wiped off her face, swallowing the mouthful of sticky sweetness as quickly as possible.

"What *happened* to you?" Rowdy asked, eyes round.

"I'm sorry about tonight, Rowdy. I was looking forward to it all day. Tractor got a flat tire in the middle of nowhere. To make things worse, I left my phone in the break room at the ranch, so I couldn't call for help. Or your mom. Took me an hour to walk back. By then my phone was dead. I was headed your way when I saw your truck." He glanced at her, sitting on the stool beside her son. "You got something right here." He took a clean napkin and wiped the side of her nose.

He was sorry. He'd been stuck in the heat for over an hour. And he'd headed straight to them—to Rowdy. As far as excuses went, these were pretty damn good.

A man shouldn't smell this good when he was this dirty.

"You could have showered first," Dot said.

Toben looked down, as if only now aware of his appearance. "Guess I could have cleaned up a little."

"No shame ever came from honest hard work." The words were out before Poppy realized she was saying them. Her granddad's words. Her cheeks grew hot under his blue-eyed inspection.

"Want some ice cream?" Rowdy asked. "I got too much."

"Don't want to deprive your ma," Toben said.

Poppy rolled her eyes. "Help yourself."

Toben shifted, nudging her aside and sharing her stool. He took the spoon the waitress offered him and dug in.

She slid off the stool but the next one was taken by a well-wrinkled old man wearing an ancient cowboy hat. "Pie," the old man said to the waitress, shooting Poppy a hard glare before turning his back on her.

"Anyone would think you were afraid of me, Poppy White." Toben's soft words were teasing, but they hit a nerve.

"Here, Ma." Rowdy slid over, putting Poppy between him and Dot. "Sorry you had a rough day."

Toben shrugged. "Not too bad. Just hot." He winked at Rowdy. "But it's good now."

The look on Toben's face made Poppy's heart thump.

"Aunt Poppy was teaching us how to throw a rope," Otis said.

"A lariat," Dot corrected. "Otis was pretty good."

"He is," Poppy agreed.

"Your aunt Poppy can do all sorts of rope tricks." Toben swallowed a large spoonful of ice cream, his blue eyes meeting hers. "One of the first times we met, she showed me a trick."

Poppy's eyes went round.

"What happened?" Rowdy asked.

"I kept trying to get your ma to go on a date with me," Toben said. "She was stubborn—kept turning me down and ignoring me."

"You did?" Rowdy frowned at her.

"She took rodeo seriously. And once I figured that out, I realized I could get her attention." He grinned. "I asked her to help me get better with my throw." He laughed, shaking his head.

"He knew how to throw just fine." Poppy joined in then, smiling in spite of herself.

"After fifteen minutes, she figured out what I was up to and got all riled up. And when she started to walk away, I lassoed her." Toben was still smiling when he finished.

"Is that when you changed your mind about him?" Dot asked.

Poppy shook her head. "No."

"That was a couple years later," Toben added. "I was determined."

Poppy tore her gaze from his. She remembered it all too well. She'd been fuming. She'd never known a man so manipulative, infuriating and cocky. And yet his smile and laugh had been impossible to ignore altogether.

"Too bad it didn't work out," Otis said. "You seem like a nice guy."

"Mitchell's a nice guy, too," Dot said. "And he's stayed with Aunt Poppy forever."

"Mitchell's a good friend to Ma and me," Rowdy said.

Toben's spoon clattered against the empty glass bowl, drawing all eyes his way. "Sorry." He grinned.

But he didn't look the least bit repentant.

"My stomach hurts," Otis groaned.

"Sounds like it's time to head home," Poppy said, hopping off the stool.

"You wanna come out?" Rowdy asked. "Have coffee on the porch? Ma likes it."

Poppy sighed, knowing what Toben's answer would be and hoping Rowdy wouldn't be too disappointed.

"That's too good an offer to refuse." Toben stood, smiling down at her, a sparkle in his eye. "Unless your ma says no." His brows rose, a silent question.

With all three of the kids—and the old man on the stool beside them—staring at her, she didn't really have a choice. "Sure. Coffee sounds good." But the flutter in her stomach told her she might not be as upset about his maneuverings as she should be.

TOBEN WAS ASLEEP on his feet. He should have gently refused Rowdy's offer, driven back to the ranch, showered and fallen into his bunk. Instead he was driving farther away from the ranch, bleary-eyed and aching.

But he followed his son inside the house, listened to him chatter as he made the coffee and managed to keep up some sort of conversation until a steaming cup was placed in front of him. He knocked it back, uncaring that it burned his throat and the roof of his mouth. He was about to pass out at the table.

"Another cup?" Rowdy asked.

"Keep it coming," he agreed.

He saw Poppy walk through the kitchen, the floor creaking as she went, carrying a full laundry basket. Her hair was down, swinging between her shoulders. And she was humming, soft and sweet.

"Ma's pretty," Rowdy said, sitting beside him at the table.

"I think so," Toben agreed.

"Why didn't you marry her?" Rowdy asked.

Toben stared at his son. It was the last question he'd expected him to ask. "Honest?"

Rowdy nodded.

"I was an idiot." He sipped his coffee. If he'd spent less time partying and living in the moment, he might have realized what was right in front of him—what he'd lose.

Rowdy sighed.

"Is there anything else you want to ask me?" Toben asked, aware that this might not be as straightforward as he hoped.

Rowdy thought about it, his face scrunched up in concentration. "You don't rodeo anymore, like Ma. Did you get hurt like she did? Or decide you were done?"

Toben was awake then. "Your mom got hurt?"

Rowdy nodded. "Broke three ribs, punctured her lung, had her right arm in a sling for a long time," he said. "Still hurts sometimes." He leaned forward to whisper. "She doesn't like that I notice that."

"She likes to be strong," Toben agreed.

"She is strong."

"That she is." Toben stared at his son. "I was done. I'll still ride for special events but I'm too old. I figure it's time for me to settle down."

"You married?" Rowdy asked.

"Nope."

Rowdy paused. "And I'm your only kid?"

"Just you, kid."

Rowdy grinned. "Girlfriend?"

Toben shook his head.

"How many Boones are there?"

"Lots," Toben asked. "I was hoping to introduce you to a few of them tonight, but that didn't quite work out." He winked. "You can meet them all Thursday night. If you want?"

Rowdy nodded. "Think they'll like me?"

Toben ruffled his son's curls. "I know they will."

"Rowdy." Poppy's voice interrupted them. "It's almost ten."

"Bedtime?" Toben asked.

"Nine," Rowdy said. "Guess she's breaking the rules tonight," he whispered, then said, "Coming, Ma."

Toben hugged Rowdy tight. "Thanks for the coffee."

"Thanks for the talk," Rowdy said.

"You think of more questions, I'll give you the answers."

"'Night…Dad." Rowdy winked at him, then hurried from the kitchen.

Toben's heart was so full. He ran a hand along the back of his neck and stole a look at the woman in the doorway. Poppy smiled at Rowdy as he brushed past, her unfiltered love for their son a thing to see.

He stood, finishing off his cup of coffee, and washed out the cup before he leaned against the counter.

"You need a shower and a bed," Poppy said.

He nodded. "I'll get out of your hair."

"You…you can stay. There's room. You'd have your own room. If you want?" She shifted from foot to foot.

"I don't mind a roommate now and then." Sleeping in a bunkhouse meant that was more the norm than the exception.

"Oh, I know." Her tone was tight and edged with temper. Her face told him she'd interpreted his comment in a completely different way. "Wouldn't want to mess up plans for later on this evening."

He chuckled. Was she jealous? He liked it. More than a little. "Nine times out of ten, I sleep in a bunkhouse on the ranch, Poppy." He watched her posture ease, her expression clear. "And, just so we're clear, I haven't had *plans* since you came to Stonewall Crossing." He saw the slight smile she wore and wondered at it. "Nice to know you care."

"I do not care. Rowdy'd be devastated if you wrecked on your way home." She crossed her arms , avoiding his gaze.

He crossed the room until they were so close he could see the unsteady rise and fall of her chest. "But you'd be okay with it?"

She stared up at him, blinking rapidly. She stepped back but there was nowhere to go. "W-with what?" Her words wavered.

He shook his head, his hand unsteady as he reached for her.

"Toben." Her tone was soft, but he heard the plea.

He stopped, his gaze pinning hers.

"We're not going to do this," she said. "We're different people. This is a different world. One I've worked hard to give me and Rowdy."

"No room for me?" he asked, trying to keep it light— even if her words hurt.

"You're his father." She stepped around him. "I'm not going to interfere."

He sighed and spun to face her. She wanted to pretend this didn't exist? That this attraction between the two of them would fade? Maybe it would. That would be a damn shame. He'd been attracted to women before, too many. But nothing compared to the spark between him and Poppy.

God knows he'd spent plenty of time hoping that wasn't the case.

She was right about Rowdy. He was the boy's father. He wanted to be that father. Looking at Poppy, he couldn't help but wonder what it would be like to give the whole family thing a real chance. The shit that used to make him run for the hills sounded almost...tempting.

"We should work out a visitation arrangement," Poppy was saying, pushing out the screen door and stepping onto the porch. "A schedule—"

"You think that's necessary?" He followed, staring at her, waiting.

She glanced at him. "I don't know. I don't know what you want."

He moved to her side, staring out over the small ranch she was intent on making her own. He swallowed back what he wanted to say. She'd bolt like a green bronc if he told her he wanted to be a part of this—all of this. And maybe, just maybe, a part of her life, too.

Hell, realizing that made him want to bolt.

"I want to be a part of Rowdy's life. Not once a week or on holidays and weekends. I want to see him first thing in the morning on a Monday for no reason. I want to take him to school. I want to help him with homework, watch him grow." He looked at her then. "I don't know how *you* want me to do that. All I know is that's what I want."

Poppy looked up at him. "I know Rowdy would like that."

"What about you, Poppy? Is a quiet family life going to be enough for you?" He turned, leaning against the porch railing. "The girl I knew wanted to rodeo until the day she died. She had big dreams and a plan to make them happen. Nothing and no one was going to stop that. I figured that out real quick."

Her brow furrowed. "You did? After hounding me for three years? After using every trick in the book to catch my attention and making me feel like a fool over and over again, turning my head one minute only to take some pretty sweet thing home for the night? I don't know how you turned what happened between us into something that happened to you." She pressed her hands flat on the porch railing. "I did have dreams, dreams I fulfilled. But the motivation wasn't the same. I had nothing and no one to help me with the baby boy placed in my arms the second I rode out of the arena. He replaced every other dream I had. Making sure he has a good, stable life is the best dream I can offer Rowdy."

Her words rocked Toben to his core. He knew she'd lost her parents, knew the grandparent who raised her had challenged her riding every step of the way, fearing she'd end up like her daddy. It made sense that with Rowdy, giving him love and acceptance was all that mattered to her now.

He respected her all the more for it.

"Let me help. I can't go back and change things, even if I wish I could. I wasn't there in the beginning, but I'm here now." He ran a hand along the back of his neck.

"I... For how long?" she whispered.

He stilled. In the grand scheme of things, it was a fair question.

"Being part of his everyday life isn't a small thing, Toben. And I never pegged you as a commitment man." She spoke a little louder now.

"I wasn't." Those images of Mitchell with Rowdy and Poppy sprang up again. "Is that why you're with Mitchell?"

"I *never* said I was *with* Mitchell." She shook her head, leveling a glare his way. "You are incredible! Mitchell is a friend—my best friend, period. Not that my personal life is any of your business—"

"Bullshit." He raised an eyebrow. "If it affects my son, it's my business." But he couldn't deny how damn happy her words made him.

"You can't be serious." Her mouth fell open. Then she laughed. "I don't have the time or energy to monitor who goes home with you."

"So you'd be okay with Rowdy knowing about my past?" he asked. And it was his past now—not the distant past, more like two weeks ago. But he didn't miss it—the women, the hangovers or the inability to fill the ache deep inside.

"I'm not going to lie to him, if that's what you're asking. I'll admit I'm hoping he doesn't ask." She stepped closer. "But if you ever, I mean ever, introduce him to one of your saddle tramps, there will be a reckoning."

Toben smiled down at her. "So you do understand?"

"Mitchell isn't a one-night stand, Toben. He's not someone I get fall-down drunk with or make a scene over. He's a good—"

"Yeah, yeah, he's a good man. We've gone over this before." Anger warmed him. "I don't know him. All I know is he sleeps under your roof, throws a mean right hook and feels the need to protect you and Rowdy. From *me*." His brows rose. "I've seen you two together, Poppy. He might be your best friend but that man wants more."

Poppy's eyes narrowed, her lips pressed tight.

He reached down, cupping her cheek in his palm and running his thumb across her lower lip. He sucked in a breath, watching his thumb, savoring the soft skin against his calluses. "He might be a good man, but he doesn't set you on fire the way you should be." His gaze locked with hers. "A woman as hungry as you are should find a man that can keep her satisfied." Her lips parted as she swayed, ever so slightly, into him.

He couldn't do it. He wanted to, so bad it hurt not to pull

her close and show her just how much he wanted her. But her words had stirred up too many doubts. There wasn't room for doubts, not now. For Rowdy's sake.

"I'll go take that shower now." His voice was gruff. "Thanks for the offer of a bed."

Even after he'd showered and he lay in Poppy's guest bed surrounded by moving boxes, he could still feel her lip against his thumb.

Chapter Eight

Poppy tossed and turned, punching her pillow into submission and fighting with her blankets until she gave up. It didn't matter that it was three in the morning—she was done pretending to sleep. If Toben Boone was trying to drive her to distraction, he was doing a damn fine job. His touch had thrilled her, sending her into a state of anticipation. His thumb had seemed to have a direct line to every nerve ending in her body. When he'd stroked her lip...

She kicked back the sheets, letting the cool morning air take some of the heat out of her blood. Damn him. Damn her for reacting to him. Why did she react to him? And how the hell did she stop?

She pulled on her work clothes, slammed her hat on her head and slipped outside. Stretching her side, easing the dull ache of her old wound, she inspected her new home with satisfaction. She threw a blanket on Stormy's back and rode along the fence line that circled the length of the house and yard. Her flashlight beam ran over the fence wire. It looked sound, barbed wire strung tight and the cedar stays strong with no signs of splitting. If she could keep her mind blank—at least Toben-free—she might get a few things done. Like marking off the plot of land she'd plant in the spring. There was no rush, except for the restlessness in the pit of her belly.

She went back to the barn in search of materials…and came up empty.

When she turned to go, she paused, staring at what had been a hole in the far corner. Now it was patched up, the wood sanded smooth. She ran her fingers along the planking, pressing against the newly reinforced frame of the stall. Good, solid work.

Mitchell hadn't had time to do this…

Her gaze peered out the open doors at her house. Toben.

She swallowed the knot in her throat, fighting back the longing and hope she'd thought had long since deserted her. This wasn't for her. This was for Rowdy. Everything he did was for Rowdy. What more could she want? She refused to consider the possible answers to that question, focusing on the list of supplies she'd need from another trip to the local hardware store. This time for some yard stays and marking ribbon. And maybe some heavy-duty gardening tools. The ground was fertile, but there were plenty of rocks to slow down progress.

Cheeto whinnied, so she rubbed his neck, talking to him softly in his stall. "Don't you worry—Rowdy will be up soon enough." She checked her watch. Almost six. Good enough to start cooking…since Toben would have to get to work soon.

She rode Stormy back to the house, pulled off the blanket and halter, and let the horse free-graze. Stormy butted her with his head, blowing hard into her hair.

"I love you, too," she whispered, pressing her face against the little gray's neck. Besides Mitchell, Stormy was one of the few constants in her life. The horse was part of the family. "Gotta feed my human baby," she murmured, patting Stormy's neck before slipping in the back screen door.

Soon Poppy was flipping pancakes on the electric griddle she'd picked up during her last grocery shop. Two plates were piled high and the sun was barely up. She set the table and smoothed the tablecloth, and still no sign of life came down the hallway.

At seven Poppy was done waiting. She marched down the hall and knocked on the guest room door, pushing it open.

Toben stood, shirtless, staring at her. "Come on in."

"I made...pancakes." She wasn't so eager to hurry breakfast along. Or see him put on a shirt. In fact, she was fine just as she was. The view was incredible. Broad shoulders, a chest and stomach cut hard and lean. And the lightest dusting of hair leading down to the waistband of his jeans. "Breakfast."

"You made me breakfast?" The surprise in his gaze pulled her attention to his face.

It was a mistake. Apparently her reaction to his male perfection was making him ready and willing. There was no misunderstanding the look in his blue eyes or the tightness of his jaw.

"I made breakfast," she repeated. "For everyone."

He took one step toward her, then another. "Kids are awake?"

She shook her head.

"So you made breakfast for me." The corner of his mouth kicked up.

She shook her head, willing herself to move but staying put.

"And you came in here to wake me up?" he asked, stopping an inch away—well within touching range.

She shook her head, distracted by a long-faded scar that ran along his clavicle. "What?"

"You came in here for me?" he asked.

She nodded.

He chuckled.

"What?" She shook her head. "No. I came in here to make sure you were up. You have work and I thought you'd want—"

His lips were soft. She hadn't expected that. In the brief time they'd spent together, nothing about him had been soft or gentle. But now…she couldn't breathe.

His hand crept along her back to cradle her head. His mouth parted slowly, his tongue teasing her until she opened for him. It was a slow kiss, the sort of unhurried intentional seduction Poppy had no experience with. All she knew was she was losing… No, *losing* wasn't the right word.

She didn't mind the feel of his chest beneath her fingertips. The rapid thump of his heart under her palm felt more like a victory. His skin contracted beneath her touch, his hands tightened in her hair, and when her fingers slid into his tangled curls, his soft groan told her he might be more affected than she was.

If that was possible.

She turned away from his kiss, holding on to him until the world righted itself. Even then, she didn't let go. He pressed his forehead to hers, his unsteady breathing fanning across her temple. This was dangerous. Being held this way, savoring his smell and touch. She craved intimacy far more than sex. Not that she'd mind that either.

"Breakfast," she repeated. "Don't want you to be late for work."

He kissed her forehead, breathing deep. "Thank you." His hands and arms released her. "I'll be right there."

She lingered in the doorway, her loneliness renewed with a fierce intensity. Something about watching him dress, catching sight of his wink and crooked grin in the mirror, was oddly comforting.

"Or you can wait," he added, his smile growing.

Her cheeks were burning hot as she headed back to the kitchen.

He joined her minutes later, tucking in his long-sleeved button-down into his work jeans. "Smells good."

She poured him a cup of coffee and put a stack of pancakes, bacon and two fried eggs on his plate.

"A man could get used to this," he said, leveling her with another crooked grin.

She shook her head, standing awkwardly at the counter.

"Not gonna eat with me?" he asked, taking a large bite of his breakfast.

She fidgeted.

"Sit down, Poppy, please. Have coffee with me." He sat back in his chair, waiting.

She sighed, sitting with her cup clutched between both hands. "You work on the family ranch?" Filling the silence was a necessity. Might as well learn some of what he'd been doing with himself for the last few years.

He nodded. "My uncle's turned most of the operations over to his kids—my cousins. Each of them has some stake. Hunter operates the working ranch, for the most part. They have cattle and partner with the State Agriculture Department to track and monitor whitetail populations, too."

Poppy was impressed.

"Archer runs an animal refuge on his acreage. He's a horse fanatic, talks to them like people. His wife has the gift, as well. It's an amazing thing to see—bet Rowdy'd get a kick out of visiting them."

"He would," she agreed. "So what do you do?"

"Whatever they need." He swallowed down his coffee. "Some days I'm driving to pick up horses for Archer, others I'm fixing windmills. This weekend we'll be vaccinating cattle."

"There's a lot of work involved in running a ranch." She

had no experience with that. "Grandpa's farm wasn't much of a farm. A couple of cows and pigs, some chickens and a donkey so mean the mailman wouldn't deliver to our place for fear of getting kicked into the next county."

Toben laughed.

"What about your family?" she asked, nervous.

He swallowed and sat back. "If you're asking about me, I'm not married. Never have been. No one waiting for me to call. And Rowdy's my only kid." He smiled. "If you're asking about the Boones, well, that would make me late for work." He stood. "Thank you for the breakfast, Poppy. I don't think I've ever had such an agreeable morning."

She rolled her eyes.

"I mean it." His gaze wandered over her face, lingering on her mouth just long enough to make her a little light-headed. "Damn but you make it hard for a man to leave."

She blinked, processing his words long after his truck had disappeared through her gate.

"Morning, Ma." Rowdy stumbled into the kitchen, his little eyes puffy and his curls sticking out every which way. "Smells good."

She pulled him into her lap, knowing he was too sleepy to argue much. "I made you pancakes."

"Where's Dad?" he asked.

Her heart thudded. She didn't mind hearing Rowdy call Toben Dad. She liked it. "He went to work." And she'd forgotten to thank him for the work he'd done in the barn. But then, she'd been a little distracted.

"He eat? Breakfast is the most important meal of the day," he said, yawning widely.

"No, I cooked all this food but I didn't let him eat a bite," she teased, tickling him until he was gasping for breath—nearly falling out of her lap.

"I love you, Ma," Rowdy said. "I'm glad we're here. I'm glad we found Dad."

She kissed his cheek, replaying the morning and Toben's parting words. Maybe he was right. This had been a very good morning. "I love you, too."

"I NEED YOU to go to El Paso." Archer didn't look up from the spreadsheet on his desk.

Toben blew out a slow breath. The last thing he wanted was a road trip, not when things were going so well with Rowdy—and Poppy.

"Got two pregnant mares. One is stuck and the other won't leave. They're mustangs—the herd was auctioned off earlier this week but they were missed somehow. I'd go anticipating a struggle." Archer sat back, running a hand over his face. "I've tried to get John Georgesson and Hildie Evans to go, but they're not free. I know this isn't the best time for you, but these animals need our help."

Archer never offered more information than was necessary. So his concession for Toben's situation meant a great deal. "I'll go," he agreed. He might not want to go, but it was what responsible adults did—their job.

"I appreciate it," Archer said. "Might be good to take another set of hands. See if Deacon's up for it."

"Be back soon." Toben saw Archer's nod and knew that was all the acknowledgment he'd get. He left the refuge administration offices, smiling at Archer's pretty wife coming down the path with their daughters.

"Toben." Archer's daughter Ivy waved, lifting a basket. "We brought Daddy some muffins I made."

Toben crouched, sniffing the basket. "Mm, smells good, Ivy. I'm sure he'll eat them up."

"Looks like a storm coming in. Hope whatever you're

up to keeps you close to home," Eden said, nodding at the clouds gathering on the horizon.

"Heading to El Paso. With any luck, I'll miss it." He tipped his hat at them, lightly tapped little Lily on her button nose and set off in search of Deacon. After walking the length of the sheds, through the paddock toward the walker wheels and past the new barn containing the rehabilitation pool, he found him. Deacon sat on a bale of hay, watching two horses. "Is that Fester?" Toben asked, sitting by his cousin.

"Watching him reminds me that anything's possible. Look at him. He's a different horse." Deacon shook his head, watching how carefully he treated the little paint.

Toben remembered all too well how mean-spirited Fester had been—he'd been the recipient of one too many bites. But once they'd put Fester and Miss Kitty together, he'd calmed. Archer thought it was because the big stallion liked taking care of other animals. Eden thought Fester just needed Miss Kitty. Whatever it was, the black horse made sure the blind paint horse was never alone.

"Gotta run?" Deacon asked.

"El Paso. I know you're champing to get on the road, but think you could take a detour with me first?" Toben stretched his arms over his head, eyeing the skies again. "Better get these two into the barn before that hits."

Miss Kitty didn't like storms. Which meant Fester didn't like storms.

After Toben and Deacon had the horses secured, they loaded up one of the Boone trucks with provisions and attached a horse trailer. Deacon checked the tire pressure, Toben checked the engine fluid levels and they piled into the truck.

"You drive. I know Archer doesn't trust me," Toben said.

Deacon shot him a look. "Normally that'd be enough to make you want to drive."

Toben smiled, pulling his phone from his pocket. He selected Poppy's number and held the phone up to his ear.

"Don't tell me you're calling her?"

"No point in looking back, Deacon," he explained. "I want to move forward with Rowdy in my life. Poppy's a part of that."

The phone rang and rang, but she didn't answer. When her voice message popped up, he cleared his throat. "Hey, Poppy, I wanted to let Rowdy know I'm going to El Paso to pick up some horses for work. If we drive through, I'll be back for Thursday-night dinner. I'll pick you up around five. If you need me, call me…" He hesitated, wanting to say more but having no idea what that might be. "Bye."

"You didn't come home last night," Deacon said, eyeing him.

Toben looked at him. "Keeping tabs on me?"

Deacon shook his head. "Hell, no. That'd be a full-time job."

They drove in silence, the rain falling in hard sheets by the time they were on the highway. The rain kicked up, requiring them to pull off onto the wide shoulder of the road and wait. Deacon turned off the windshield wipers and found a weather report on the radio.

The radio announcer's voice filled the truck cabin. "Expect hail and heavy rains on and off through the rest of the morning, then things will warm up into the triple digits. For now, batten down the hatches and hold on tight—things are going to get bumpy."

"Well, this sucks," Deacon said, leaning forward to peer out the front windshield. "Not gonna make Archer happy." He turned the engine off, sighing heavily.

"Even he can't control the weather." Toben chuckled.

Deacon laughed, too, then tilted his seat back and pushed his hat down over his face.

"Sleeping?" Toben asked.

"Thinking about it." His voice was muffled under his hat.

"I kissed her," he said. "This morning."

Deacon lifted his hat. "That where you slept last night?"

"In a guest bed, alone," Toben elaborated.

Deacon grinned. "So you're not mad at her anymore?"

Toben looked at his lock screen. It was a picture from last night: Rowdy with ice cream on the tip of his nose, smiling like crazy. And in the background was Poppy. "No."

"You ever been faithful?" Deacon asked.

Toben glared at him. "Never had someone to be faithful to."

Deacon pushed his hat back, leveling him with a hard stare. "Now you do?"

Toben respected Deacon. He was the sort of man who lived by his word and didn't tolerate any shit. The sort of man Toben wanted to be. For Rowdy. For himself. And, if there was even the slightest chance, for Poppy. "Now I do," he said.

Deacon grinned. "Take a lesson from Fester, then."

Toben frowned.

"He's not biting people and causing drama anymore. Making his little lady happy makes him happy. Simple." Deacon yawned.

Toben nodded.

"This is gonna be fun to watch."

Toben scowled at his cousin. It wasn't going to be simple, but nothing worth getting was ever easy. To Toben, there was nothing worth getting more than his family.

Chapter Nine

Over the last two days, Toben had sent them pictures. Funny captions, he and his cousin Deacon making all sorts of silly faces, and some incredible scenery. When her phone went off, all three kids gathered to see what he'd sent next.

A picture of Deacon asleep in the driver's seat read "Wishing I'd offered to drive." Another of Toben and Deacon standing in front of the painted hills in West Texas said "Nature's beauty at its finest. And the hills are nice, too." The picture of Toben at the end of a lasso, being dragged in a cloud of dirt, read "Toben at work." Followed by one of Deacon, sitting in the shade dozing. "Deacon at work."

The last picture he'd sent was thirty minutes ago. A picture of Toben. His jaw was stubbled and his eyes were red rimmed with dark circles. He was leaning out the passenger window, taking a picture of himself with the Boone Refuge sign in the background.

"He's back," Otis said.

"He said he'd be back." Rowdy jumped up, excited.

"Guess that means we're going to dinner?" Dot asked, but her normal bored expression was missing. "What do we wear?"

Good question. What did you wear to meet the family of the man who had fathered your only child? And what sort of reception should she expect? If the roles were reversed...

No, don't go there. She chewed the inside of her lip. Secretly, she'd been hoping Toben's trip would prevent this dinner from happening. She knew Rowdy was excited but she was terrified. These people weren't her family. Chances were, they weren't going to welcome her with open arms. They'd side with Toben—that was what family did. To them, she was the woman who'd hidden Rowdy from his father. Not the woman who'd done her best to raise her boy on her own—the woman who'd thought Toben wanted nothing to do with them.

"Be yourself, Dot. Always be yourself," Poppy said.

"You should wear a dress, Ma," Rowdy said.

"A dress?" Otis made a face. "Do you own a dress, Aunt Poppy?"

"She can't wear a dress. She just said to be yourself. Aunt Poppy wears jeans. Every day. She can't wear a dress." Dot smiled at her. "Right?"

"Ma?" Rowdy made his face—the face Poppy never said no to. He rarely used it, so when he did, it was a powerful tool.

"I'm not sure I've unpacked them," she lied, knowing the four dresses she owned were hanging in the back of her closet, behind her coats and coveralls.

The kids tore off down the hall to her room while she slumped in her chair. Could she get out of it? Was there some way she could send Rowdy alone? But he was just as nervous as she was, even if his nerves were based on excitement.

"Found one, Ma!" Rowdy called out.

She pushed out of her chair and walked, slowly, down the hall.

Dot was holding a light blue sundress. A pale pink floral knit dress, a Southwest-patterned shirtdress and an off-the-shoulder navy cotton dress were being spread across her bed by the boys.

"I like this one," Dot said, offering her the sundress.

"Pink," Rowdy said. "It's your favorite color."

"I don't think I've ever worn that one," she admitted, eyeing the far-too-feminine pink dress. What had her sister been thinking when she bought it? She wrinkled up her nose and shook her head.

"You look good in this one, Ma." Rowdy picked up the navy dress. "You wore this the day I won my first mutton-busting buckle." He pressed it into her hands. "It's good luck, I know it."

"And your sparkly boots." Dot held them up. "I've never seen them before."

Poppy smiled at Rowdy. "I wasn't planning on dressing up, Rowdy."

"You don't have to wear those boots, Ma. Your plain ones are fine." He took the boots from Dot and returned them to her closet. Apparently, he wasn't going to give up the dress.

While they hurried off to get ready, Poppy stared at the dress. She didn't want Toben thinking she was dressing for him. She wasn't. If she had it her way, she'd wear jeans and a nice button-down. But she didn't want to disappoint *Rowdy*. She wanted him to be proud of her. And if that meant she had to wear a stupid dress, she'd do it.

She showered, smoothed lotion onto her legs and slipped into the dress. It fell above her knees, revealing more skin than she was used to. She stepped into her boots and sighed. Maybe if her shoulders weren't on display...or she were wearing jeans.

"Aunt Poppy, Toben's here," Otis called.

"I'll let him in, Ma," Rowdy called out.

She stared at her reflection, so nervous she couldn't

move. She ran her fingers through her hair, then smoothed the fabric of her dress. It seemed too…little, showing far too much Poppy in the process. She shifted from foot to foot, then turned from her mirror. She added her gold locket with Grandpa's and Rowdy's pictures inside on its long chain, some gold hoops and a touch of lip gloss and forced herself from the bedroom.

"Ready?" she asked, refusing to look up. If she didn't look at him, she wouldn't see his smug smile. She wouldn't regret making Rowdy happy—because this was for Rowdy. Not Toben. But the kitchen was quiet, absolutely quiet. And the longer the silence stretched, the harder it was to keep staring at the floor.

She risked a glance up. All eyes were on her.

"You look real nice, Ma." There was pride in her son's eyes. "Thanks for wearing the dress."

"Aunt Poppy, you're so pretty." Dot was staring.

"I like you better in jeans," Otis said. "I'm hungry. Can we go?"

She didn't look at Toben.

"Yes," she said. "Let's go."

The kids ran from the kitchen, leaving her alone—with Toben. She saw his polished boots and freshly pressed and starched jeans but kept her gaze averted.

"Not going to look at me?" he asked.

She blew out a deep breath. "Not yet."

"I've got something for you," he said. "Hold out your hand."

She rolled her eyes.

"Please," he added, amusement in his voice.

She held her hand out, tensing at his coarse touch. But then he pressed something against her palm… "Flowers?" She stared at the bouquet of yellow roses, surprised.

"I remember you liked them. Yellow roses, I mean."

She stared at him then, too stunned to realize it was a bad idea.

"You look beautiful." His voice dropped. "Damn beautiful."

She swallowed, the heat and appreciation in his eyes making her feel beautiful.

"I'm glad Rowdy asked you to wear a dress." He smiled. "Guess I should check on the kids." He left her staring after him, confused and surprised and wishing the night were over. He was far too good-looking and sweet-talking. She'd ignored him before; she could do it again. Of course, then she'd given in and…giving in to Toben Boone had been one of the most amazing experiences of her life. She stiffened. One she would not be repeating.

She pulled an empty glass pitcher from the cabinet, filled it with water and put the roses inside. She stared at them, tracing one petal…thinking of the kiss she and Toben had shared. A kiss she'd thought about far too much the last couple of days. When she was working in the shop, arranging inventory or hanging pictures on the wall, Toben's touch, his kiss, was there.

Which was silly. And she wasn't a silly girl, not anymore. There was too much at stake with this man. Whatever superficial attraction the two of them had wouldn't last. A bond between father and son should last forever. No way she'd risk that for Rowdy. Or Toben.

She left the kitchen, then pulled the front door closed behind her to find all the kids in the bed of Toben's pickup, staring upward. He was pointing at something in the darkening sky, his voice deep and soft. She walked forward, listening.

"That's the Big Dipper. Can you see it?" he asked. "We can check again when we come back after dinner. By then it'll be dark enough to really see."

"Did you know the stars change with the seasons?" Rowdy asked her.

"Sure," she said. "Guess I never thought to mention it before."

"It's cool," Dot said. "And that some of the stars have stories."

"I'm still hungry," Otis said.

Toben laughed. "Load up." He helped each of them jump from the truck, then held the passenger door open for her.

"Thank you," she murmured.

"My pleasure," he answered, his eyes sweeping over her before he closed the door.

"Ma," Rowdy whispered, taking her hand over the seat back. "I'm nervous."

"Don't be, Rowdy," she answered. "They're going to love you." Of course they'd love him. Rowdy was irresistible. She smiled broadly at him, setting aside her own unease.

Toben climbed into the truck and started the engine. She reached behind her and squeezed Rowdy's hand, but he didn't let go. Toben turned the truck around and headed down the drive, through the gate and onto the county road.

"Ma," he whispered again. "You want to do this?"

She turned, looking over her shoulder. He looked... scared. Something her son rarely was. "If you're not ready, this can wait. I know your dad will understand." She looked at Toben, silently pleading for his understanding.

"Heck, yeah," Toben said, his slight nod a comfort. "We'll do this whenever you're ready. There's no rush."

Poppy breathed easier, hoping Rowdy asked for more time.

"I'm sorry," he said, sitting back against the seat. "Can... can we wait?"

"Yep." Toben stopped the truck. "We're all dressed up.

What do you want to do?" He turned, draping his arm along the seat back.

Rowdy shrugged but didn't say anything.

"You feeling okay?" She was worried. Fifteen minutes ago, he was ecstatic over tonight.

He nodded.

"I'm still hungry," Otis groaned.

"Dinner?" Poppy asked, hoping Rowdy would perk up.

"I guess," he murmured. "Not real hungry."

"Why don't you take Otis and Dot in for some chow and Rowdy and I will stay here and play some checkers or something? Since he's not feeling too social," Toben offered. "As long as you bring something back."

Rowdy sat up then. "You'll stay?"

Toben nodded, reaching out to pat Rowdy's little knee. "That's why I'm here, Rowdy. You." He looked at her. "Okay with you?"

Poppy nodded, unable to completely dismiss Rowdy's change of heart.

By the time she left Toben and Rowdy back in the house, they were already sizing up their checkerboard. She stood, watching them sprawled out across the living room floor, concentrating. When they both looked up, shooting her the same smile, the resemblance was almost painful.

"What's up?" Rowdy asked.

"You're okay?" she asked. "You two want anything in particular?"

"Food." Toben shook his head. "But take your time."

Poppy nodded, then went outside, reluctantly loading Otis and Dot into the truck and driving into town.

"You won. Again." Toben laughed. He'd thrown the first game, but not the last three. Rowdy was sharp as a tack.

"Wanna play something different?" Rowdy asked,

pulling the box of board games closer. "Mom and I play Parcheesi all the time, so I might beat you at that."

Toben pulled the Parcheesi game out. "Challenge accepted."

Rowdy laughed.

"You like board games, Cheeto, swimming and pie..." Toben lay on his side, resting on his elbow. "What else should I know?"

"I'm allergic to wasps. I hate asparagus. I like to hear my mom sing—she's really good at everything..." He paused, tapping his pointer finger against his chin. "You can ask me what you want to know."

Toben watched his son. He was his usual bouncy self, not a care in the world. But something had upset him earlier, and he didn't need Poppy's look to figure that out.

"Having a good summer?" he asked.

Rowdy made a silly face. "I met you. Course I am."

Toben's heart swelled. "What would make it better?"

"Dot and Otis leaving." Rowdy's smile faded.

Toben's suspicion was confirmed. "Don't get along?"

Rowdy shrugged, then shook his head. "I try, real hard. Ma's patient. But they're...not nice."

"To you?" he asked, arranging the Parcheesi pieces casually.

Rowdy nodded, his eyes darting from the game board to Toben and back. "They...they've said some not so nice stuff about Ma, and you, and...stuff."

Toben looked at his son. "You can tell me if you want. Sometimes having someone to talk to makes it feel less bad."

"I don't want you to get mad." He sucked in his breath. "Or leave."

Toben's instinct was to react, but he didn't want to stop

Rowdy from talking. Even if his guts were churning. "You worry I'll leave?"

Rowdy shook his head, then nodded. "I don't want to."

"But you do?"

"Dot said you didn't want us. Her folks say Ma's gonna always be alone and I'll never have a real family." Rowdy's chin quivered. "And Otis said you might go back to not wanting us if...if your family doesn't like me. Or Ma." A big tear rolled down his cheek.

Toben's heart broke at the sight of that tear. He could be mad later, but not right now. "I need to tell you something, Rowdy." He cleared his throat, looking at his son.

Rowdy wiped his nose with the back of his hand, his brown eyes filling anew.

"I'm not leaving you. Ever. I'm your dad and I love you." He smiled. "My uncle Teddy's a good man. He has five kids and a bunch of grandkids—some born to him, some that came through marriage. And you know what? It doesn't matter. That love is theirs. That family is theirs. And that family, my family, is yours. Because you're my boy. I can tell you right now, they're lucky to have you. I know I am."

Rowdy smiled. "You are?"

It was Toben's turn to make a disbelieving face. "I am. The day I saw your ma again I knew my life had changed for the better."

"Ma's like that," Rowdy agreed.

Toben laughed. "She is."

"We're lucky to have her." Rowdy picked up the dice in one hand. "I'm sorry about tonight."

He shook his head. "No need, Rowdy. As long as I get time with you, I'm good." But he wasn't done. "I think maybe Dot and Otis are hurting inside, missing their folks. I guess they want other people to hurt, too. I'm not saying it's right, but some people are wired that way." His own mother was a perfect example.

Rowdy frowned. "I'm not."

"I'm glad." Another reason to thank Poppy. "Now you need to teach me how to play so I can win."

Rowdy laughed, then scooched onto his stomach to explain the rules.

By the time Poppy arrived, Toben was starving.

"Food," Poppy called from the kitchen.

Rowdy jumped up and ran into the other room.

"Hold up—it's my turn." Toben dropped the dice and followed him into the kitchen.

Poppy smiled as she set three places at the dinner table. Dot and Otis stood, shoulder to shoulder, looking downright pathetic. Toben tried not to grin. So he wasn't the only one who'd figured out what happened tonight. From the looks of it, they'd already received quite a talking-to.

"Dot and Otis have something they need to say to you, Rowdy," Poppy said.

Rowdy looked at his cousins.

"We're sorry," Dot said. "For the things we said."

"Yeah," Otis echoed. "I shouldn't have said your dad might leave."

"It's okay." Rowdy sat at the table and unwrapped his burger without hesitation. "I forgive you."

Poppy looked at him, her smile surprised.

Toben sat beside Rowdy and unwrapped his food, too.

"Good night, you two. And no games or they're mine." Poppy watched them walk down the hall. The guest room door shut with more force than necessary. "Aunt Rose will be here soon." She squeezed Rowdy's shoulder.

"She keep them in line?" Toben took a sip. "Milk shake? Good call."

Poppy's smile lit her up. "I thought we could all use a good drink." She winked at Rowdy.

"You're the best." Rowdy took a long pull off his straw. "Dad and I agree on that."

"Is that the milk shake talking?" Poppy asked.

Rowdy laughed. "No. We were saying that before you got home."

"Oh, well, then I guess that's nice." She ruffled Rowdy's curls and sat back in her chair with a sigh.

"Tired?" he asked.

She looked pointedly down the hall. "Very." Her phone started to ring.

Toben watched her glance quickly at him, then back at the phone. He knew who it was but he didn't know why it bothered him. If anything, his run-in with Mitchell had taught him to respect the other man. He clearly cared about Poppy and Rowdy and had for some time. Not that Toben liked it. Not one bit. He cleared his throat, trying to sound unaffected. "You going to answer that?"

"Mitchell?" Rowdy asked.

Toben took a long sip of his milk shake—wishing it was a beer.

"Mitchell calls when he's on the road." Rowdy scooped ketchup onto his fry. "He's been all over, emceeing rodeos. They have rodeos in Scotland."

Toben shook his head. "I didn't know that. That sounds interesting."

She muted the phone and set it down. "I'm too hungry to talk right now." Which suited him just fine.

He watched as she tucked her long brown curls over her shoulder, resisting the urge to smooth one rebellious strand behind her ear. She was far too graceful for such a no-frills, no-fuss woman. When she moved, he was mesmerized. Toben finished his burger, tried not to stare and listened to the easy conversation between mother and son.

Rowdy was full of such energy and joy. He pulled Toben into the conversation, too. Asking him questions about his favorite rodeo arena, favorite bull and favorite ride. Toben answered, just as eager to fill in some of the blanks as Rowdy seemed to be. His son's grin, his laugh, the confidence on his young face—watching Rowdy filled Toben with hope. Maybe they could be a family. Maybe this was his chance to be the kind of father he never had.

"You know why a frog is always happy?" Rowdy asked.

He and Poppy shook their heads.

"He eats what's bugging him." Rowdy paused, looking back and forth between them. "Get it? Eats what's *bugging* him?"

Toben chuckled. Poppy threw back her head, laughing. God, she was beautiful. His gaze slid along her long neck, the slope of her exposed shoulder and the line of her collarbone. He swallowed. She had some sort of power over him—making him sit up, take notice and…want.

He was good at that: wanting things he couldn't have.

Once dinner was over, he and Rowdy reset the game so Poppy could join in.

"Prepare to lose," Poppy said, kicking off her boots and sitting on a pillow on the ground.

"It's good to dream, Ma. Isn't that what you say?" Rowdy asked, giggling.

Toben shook his head and sat across from them, intrigued by their banter. He'd never had this sort of relationship with a parent. And his mother would certainly never have sat on the floor to play a game with him and his sister. Her lack of motherly affection and attention was all he'd known. By the time he left home, his mother had "warned" both his uncles that Toben was a handful and Tandy too sweet for her own good. Uncle Woodrow had tolerated them, but his suspicious and harsh nature was too much for him. They'd left the West Texas ranch and headed straight to Stonewall Crossing. Thankfully, Uncle Teddy had welcomed them with open arms and Toben had found home.

Poppy smiled as Rowdy lay back, his head in her lap. Her fingers slid through the boy's curls, gently separating tangles and stroking his temple. It was soothing to watch. He could only imagine how amazing it would feel. He had no doubt that was why Rowdy fell asleep long before the game was over.

"Can I help?" Toben asked when she started to lift their son.

She nodded, letting him carry Rowdy down the hall and into the boy's bedroom. He held his son close, studying each feature. His fine brows, the slight tilt of his nose, his long eyelashes and his solid weight in Toben's arms. When Poppy pulled back the covers, he didn't want to release him.

He stooped, brushing the boy's curls from his forehead to kiss his brow. He straightened, staring down at him. He'd never felt this way, such pride and hope at what they'd do together, frustration and sorrow at what he'd missed.

Poppy tugged off Rowdy's boots while Toben stared around the room. Rowdy had a range of things tacked to his wall. He was proud of his rodeoing and the folk he came from. Ribbons and belt buckles were displayed on racks in Plexiglas covers. On the wall were a few newspaper clippings. Pictures of Poppy's dad in his bull-riding gear. A picture of an old man standing by a pasture fence, clearly irritated at having his picture taken. More pictures of Poppy in the ring. Rowdy, covered in dirt, holding up a ribbon. A picture of Poppy on Stormy, midride and working. And a press shot... He stepped closer, staring at the framed photo. A younger, cockier version of himself smiled back. Close-cropped hair, sporting a pathetic beard and patchy mustache, his lucky hat tucked under his arm. All brash and ego—that Toben had nothing to lose and no care in the world. His goal in life had been to win enough to get the women and earn enough to pay for the party. He read the words written by his own hand and felt sick. "Good Luck and Hold On Tight! —Toben Boone."

I sent you letters. Letter after letter. Left messages with every woman that answered your phone—left messages so you could reach me. And you sent me an autographed picture.

Poppy's words filled his ears. His heart lodged in his throat. Tears burned his eyes. He couldn't move. How many letters had he thrown away unread? How many messages had he deleted unheard? She'd tried to tell him. *This* was his answer.

"Toben?" Poppy whispered.

He shook his head, fighting the urge to smash his cocky picture into dust. Hate, sadness and near-crippling shame grabbed him by the throat and refused to let go.

She stood next to him, close enough she could whisper. "He loves that picture."

He glanced at his son, fighting tears, and hurried from Rowdy's room. The walls seemed to press in on him. Poppy's words, what she'd tried to tell him… He hadn't really believed her, hadn't wanted to believe her. He was the one who'd been wronged. He was the one who hadn't known about his son… Maybe he hadn't, but he was beginning to accept it wasn't from *her* lack of trying. She'd sent a letter—one of the many letters he never took the time to read—a letter that told him she was expecting his child.

He'd replied with that?

He pushed out the back door, sucking in fresh air. He was an asshole. A selfish sonofabitch.

"Toben?" He heard the crunch of her boots on the gravel behind him.

He held his hand up, shaking his head. He couldn't talk, not yet, or he'd fall apart.

"What's wrong?"

"I need to go," he said.

"Okay." She followed him to his truck.

He pulled open the truck door, desperate for space.

"Toben, wait, please."

He did. But looking at her, facing her, was hard.

"I just wanted to say thank you." She was rubbing her arms, her bare shoulders. "For tonight."

He slammed the truck door. "Thank me?" He ran a hand along the back of his neck. "Dammit, Poppy. Don't thank me. Get mad at me. Hate me. Shit."

Poppy frowned. "You want me to hate you?"

He pointed at the house. "No. I don't want you to hate me. It's what I deserve." He shook his head and pulled the truck door open. He couldn't do this, couldn't face her, not right now. He turned on the engine and drove away as fast as he could—angrily wiping at his eyes.

Chapter Ten

"It's certainly a fixer-upper, now, isn't it?" Rose stood in the middle of the kitchen, a mix of horror and sympathy on her still-too-thin face. "I guess I can see the potential. But, wow, there's a lot to be done."

Poppy didn't argue. She liked the white walls, wide-wood-plank flooring and large windows that let in natural light. But there was a fair amount of work to do. From the appliances to the plumbing, new lighting fixtures and a curtain here or there...

"What's wrong with it?" Bob asked, hands on his hips, already radiating impatience. "Stove, fridge, microwave, sink, dishwasher. It's a kitchen."

Poppy pressed her lips tight, refusing to smile. She'd always found Bob's directness amusing. Rose, however, was unimpressed.

"Did you look at the stove? Honestly, Bob—"

"The fire alarm has gone off lots," Otis offered. "But the chicken wasn't burned. Aunt Poppy makes good fried chicken."

Rose frowned at her. "Fire alarm?"

"It's an old stove, Rose. The element smokes something fierce. New one should be here in a few days." Poppy sighed, staring out the window at the wavering skyline. It was hot. So hot the air seemed to shimmer and sway. "Just a little smoke and a lot of noise."

"We figured out how to turn it off with a broom handle." Dot was proud of this. "We've had ice cream. And painted the bathroom in Aunt Poppy's shop. We learned to ride Cheeto. Oh, and we swam in the river, too."

Poppy looked at her niece with an approving smile. The girl had a golden hue to her skin. The last week they'd spent a lot of time at the shop and even more time outside. Both Dot and Otis seemed more comfortable around the horses. And they weren't squeamish about catching grasshoppers for fishing bait anymore—a big victory in her eyes. Putting them on a fishing hook was another matter.

"Swimming in the river?" Bob asked.

"Right down the hill behind the house," Otis said. "Wanna go? It's a scorcher out there."

"A scorcher, huh?" Bob found this hilarious.

"Toben said that," Dot offered. "He says all sorts of cowboy-y things."

She glanced at Rowdy, noting his glum expression and knowing why. Any mention of his father upset him. Toben had driven away three days ago and had not bothered to send a text or call his son. He'd left Rowdy to draw his own conclusions about why he'd suddenly disappeared—something that made her want to give Toben Boone a talking-to. Not that it would help. Poppy knew the truth. Toben was scared. He'd been fine when it was all fun and games. But as soon as it got serious, as soon as it got real, he'd bolted. That picture had been too much for the man. Nothing like seeing how devoted his boy was to freak him out. Toben Boone knew nothing about commitment or loyalty.

She ruffled Rowdy's hair, glancing at her sister. Rose's eyes were round and her mouth hung open. Poppy knew it was too much to hope the topic of Toben wouldn't come up over their weekend visit, but she'd hoped, anyway. She wasn't going to talk about Toben with her sister. She would smile, chat and make sure the next forty-eight hours were as pleasant and conflict-free as possible. "A swim sounds like a good idea, Otis."

"Too bad Toben's not here to throw us," Dot said, leading the charge down the hall, the sound of slamming doors echoing all the way into her clean, white-walled kitchen.

"Kids look good," Bob said. "Thanks, Poppy."

"You two look good." Poppy pointed at them. "Rested. Refreshed."

Bob placed an arm around Rose's shoulders. "Long overdue. Might have to turn this into an annual thing—for you and the kids."

Poppy smiled. Dot and Otis would fight it every year, but she wouldn't mind. She hoped that, in time, the cousins would forge a bond that would hold their small family together.

"Are they talking about *that* Toben? Toben Boone? *Rowdy's father?*" Rose asked. "You can't tell me *he's* here?"

"He lives here." Poppy shrugged.

"Oh, Poppy… That's not why…" Rose glanced at Bob, then leaned forward, whispering, "That's not why you picked Stonewall Crossing is it? To be close to him? Tell me it's not."

"It's not." She sighed. "Did you bring your swimsuits?"

"Yep." Bob took his suitcase handle.

"So I'm supposed to believe this was some sort of accident?" Rose asked, crossing her arms over her chest. "It's a little too convenient, don't you think?"

Poppy sighed again. "I wanted to move here. I'd been through this sweet town a time or two when I was still riding. It's… I don't know… It feels like home." That had been all the reason she'd needed to trust the property agent to find her the perfect spread. That he'd found a place in less than three weeks told her this was where she and Rowdy were meant to be.

Until Toben Boone showed up on her front porch.

Rose put her hands on Poppy's shoulders. "Did he explain why he's ignored his own son all this time? Are you letting him see Rowdy?"

Poppy brushed aside her sister's touch. "We're working the details out as we go along. So far, so good. Let's get the kids to the river and enjoy the day."

"I'm so sorry you're having to go through this again," Rose said, her pale brown eyes glistening. "He's already hurt you two enough. It doesn't seem right. Is Rowdy okay?"

Poppy nodded, lying. Right now Rowdy was not okay. And she didn't know what to do about it.

"We're in the last bedroom?" Bob asked, steering the wheeled suitcase and Rose to the hallway.

"On the right," Poppy said.

She stood at the sink, staring out the window, wishing there was a way to fast-forward the weekend. She loved Rose, and she'd wanted to show her sister all the delights of Stonewall Crossing. But now she wondered if that was wise.

"Ma?" Rowdy's voice. "You coming?"

She spun around, smiling. "Yes, sir."

He wrinkled up his nose. "Like that?"

She looked down at her jeans and shirt. "Nope." She smiled. "Give me a sec." She hurried to change, worried about Rose talking to Rowdy one-on-one. She slipped into her modest two-piece, tugged on an old button-down work shirt and hurried back to the kitchen.

Her phone rang, making Rowdy perk up.

"Hi, Mitchell," she answered, winking at her son. His disappointment was obvious.

"Hey, yourself. You sound…funny." The connection crackled. "Not the best service out here, I guess."

"Where are you headed?" she asked.

"We ready?" Bob emerged alone. "Rose is going to rest."

"That Toben?" Mitchell asked, sounding cool and calm.

"No." She held up her finger and walked onto the front porch. "Been a few days."

"Surprise," Mitchell growled. "So who's there?"

"Rose and Bob."

"Guess that means the guest bed's taken?" he asked.

She smiled, staring out over the pasture. "The couch is soft."

"Sold," he said. "I'll be there in a few hours. You okay?"

She blew out a deep breath. "Yeah, I guess."

"Don't let him get you down, Pops. He's not worth your time or tears."

Mitchell was always on her side. "Is that from a song?" she asked.

"Is it? Might be. If not, I'll write one." He laughed. "See you soon."

"Be safe," she said before hanging up.

Mitchell was very good at cheering Rowdy up. Something her boy needed right now. If she was being honest, he was also a great buffer between her and Rose. Everyone liked Mitchell Lee. Everyone. If she were smart, she'd like him more. Mitchell would never run out on his wife and kid. When his first wife left him—not long before Poppy had finally received Toben's picture in the mail—he'd been a sad sort. The two of them had bonded over heartbreak and built each other up, cementing a solid friendship in the process. She didn't know how she'd have survived without him.

"Can we go?" Rowdy asked.

"Definitely," Poppy said. "Got the sunblock?"

Dot held up the bottle.

"Water bottles," Otis said, holding them up.

"Towels," Rowdy said, pointing at Bob and his load of towels.

"Looks like we're ready," she said, picking up the inner tubes from the side of the house.

Poppy, Bob and the three kids made their way to the river—all three kids talking at once.

TOBEN STOOD ON the massive wraparound porch of Ryder Boone's home. He could hear the giggles and squeals inside. Ryder and his wife, Annabeth, had three boys—twin two-year-olds and an eight-year-old. They were loud, rambunctious kids who made his cousin burst with pride.

He knocked on the door, smiling when three voices yelled, "Door!"

"I'll get it." Annabeth was smiling, too. "You didn't have to knock, Toben. You're family, after all. Come on in." She stepped back. "Watch the toys. The place is booby-trapped."

He grinned, assessing the floor. He sidestepped a castle, dodged a mountain of teddy bears and almost tripped on a metal sports car.

"Ryder, Toben's here," Annabeth called out. To Toben she said, "Can I get you something? Lemonade? Water? Tea?"

Toben shook his head. "I'm good." He looked down, smiling at Dawson and Emmett. The twins were each clinging to one of his legs, using him as their personal ride. "Looks like I'm getting a leg workout."

"Who needs a gym?" she asked.

Toben grinned. Annabeth was a beautiful woman. His

cousin Ryder was a lucky man. He had it all, wife, kids—
he was happy.

"Send him out, will ya, Princess?" Ryder called. "With
something to drink, please, ma'am."

Annabeth poured two glasses of lemonade, handed them
to Toben and nodded at the back door. "Boys, let Uncle
Toben go help Daddy with the motorcycle."

"Where's Cody?" Toben asked, looking for their eldest.

"Shh, Uncle Toben," Cody called out. "I'm hiding."

The twins let go, running into the other room in the direction of Cody's voice, squealing.

Annabeth shook her head and followed the twins into
the front room while he headed out the back door.

Ryder's hands were black with grease. "Cousin." He nodded. "Feel like making yourself useful?" Toben nodded. He
helped Ryder for a full thirty minutes before Ryder asked,
"Wanna tell me why you're here?"

Toben wiped his hands on a shop rag and sat on the metal
stool. "I'm in deep."

Ryder downed the lemonade and stared at him. "Trou-
ble?"

Toben nodded.

"What's going on?" Ryder sat opposite Toben, wiping
his hands.

He wished he could put the jumble of emotions in his
head into words. "I don't know how to be a better man."

Ryder's brow creased. "You're asking me?"

"You and I were on similar paths." Toben glanced at the
house. "Until you met Annabeth."

Ryder stared at the house. "There's a woman?"

Toben cleared his throat. "And my son."

Ryder's blue eyes went round and he sat back. "Well,
now. When's he due?"

"He's six. I've got a lot of time to make up for...a lot to make up for. Question is, how?" He shook his head, the shame that had been sitting on his chest for three days making it hard to say a word. "What I did..." He shook his head again.

"Can't get beyond it?" Ryder asked. "If you don't let go, they can't. All you can do is start now."

Toben looked at his cousin. "Why the hell would they want me in their life?"

"You'll have to figure that out. No more feeling sorry for yourself or talking yourself out of doing what needs to be done." Ryder pointed at the house. "It's work. Every day. But, damn, is it worth it."

Toben stared at his hands, the black beneath his nails.

"You want this boy in your life?" Ryder asked.

"Yes."

"His mother?" Ryder paused. "Seems to me you don't have room for mistakes here, Toben. You need to be damn sure of what you want before you answer that one."

Poppy White. He wanted her. She seemed to flip a switch he hadn't known existed whenever she walked into the room. If he could turn it off, he should—but he couldn't. More important, he wasn't sure he wanted to. He'd spent years trying to get Poppy White into his bed. In the process, he'd let her into his heart. Thinking about it now, he wasn't sure he'd ever let her out.

But Ryder was right.

"Focus on your son. I can't imagine not seeing those boys every day, letting them know I'm their daddy and I'm proud of them." He stared into his empty glass, then smiled and reached for Toben's. "They need lots of love when they're little—to know it, feel it, believe it. Best way to do that is be there."

Toben swallowed. Could he be there, face-to-face, without his shame killing him?

"She trying to keep you from him?" Ryder asked.

He shook his head.

"Then why the hell are you here?" Ryder asked, standing.

"I can't...shake the hurt. I did this. I tore up the letters she wrote. I never returned a single damn phone call. She tried to tell me about our son, over and over, and I turned my back on her—on them. I have no right to be there," he ground out.

"Maybe you don't. But not being there tells that boy there are things that come before him." Ryder put his hands on his hips.

"That's not true." Toben stood, his irritation mounting. He hadn't come here to get an extra heap of guilt and feel worse.

"I know that. You know that. But your son— What's his name?" Ryder asked.

"Rowdy." He grinned.

Ryder's smile was broad. "Rowdy needs to know that. He comes first now. Period. If you want to be a better man, that's all you need to know and do."

Toben sucked in a deep breath.

"Is this the rodeo gal?" Ryder asked. "The one Renata wants carrying the flag in the parade."

Toben nodded. "Poppy White."

Ryder nodded. "You were sweet on her, I remember."

"Guess I still am," he mumbled.

Ryder laughed. "Start with Rowdy. Something tells me winning over your son is going to be a hell of a lot easier than winning over the woman."

Toben handed Ryder the wrench. "Thanks for the lemonade."

"Anytime. Bring him over. Rowdy. Cody's not that much older than him."

Toben waved and set off for the truck. Even though it had been only three days, he missed Rowdy something fierce. He didn't want to miss him anymore. He turned the truck and headed to the winding country road that would take him to his family.

Chapter Eleven

"The kids are wiped out," Rose said, helping Poppy load the dishwasher. "Maybe we need to get a pool."

"They do love the water." But Poppy suspected it had more to do with the hours of play, their father's involvement and the adventure they'd shared swimming up the river a ways. "You should come with us tomorrow, Rose."

"In the river?" Rose shook her head. "I've never been outdoorsy like you, Poppy. You know that."

"All you have to do is float. I have an inner tube. The kids will push you along."

"Maybe," Rose said.

"Mitchell wants some citronella candles." Bob peered in the screen door.

Poppy pulled three of the large tin candles out from under the sink. "The lighter is in the drawer," she said to Rose. "Can you get it for Bob?"

Bob retreated, carrying the candles and lighter back to the fire pit. The kids were gathered around, waiting for the s'mores supplies. Poppy grabbed a box of graham crackers, several chocolate bars and a bag of marshmallows.

"Isn't it a little late for sugar?" Rose asked, following her outside.

"Yes. But it's a treat." Poppy put the supplies down and

sat beside Rowdy on the large rocks that surrounded the fire pit. "A yummy, sticky, gooey treat."

"Are we supposed to sing songs, too?" Bob asked.

"Do you want to sing?" Mitchell asked.

"No," Otis said quickly. "Dad can't sing."

"Don't let him," Dot echoed.

"Ma can sing," Rowdy piped up.

Poppy looked at her son. "No, I can't, Rowdy."

"Sure you can," Rowdy pushed. "You used to sing to me every night. And you still do, when you're in the shower or working out in the barn. I hear you."

"Maybe I only do it then because I think no one can hear me." She laughed, smoothing the curls from his forehead.

"I like it," Rowdy said.

She wrapped her arm around him and tugged him close. "That's because you love me." She tickled his ribs until he was breathless. "How about we just stick with s'mores?"

Mitchell stripped the bark off several long branches, skewered some white fluffy marshmallows and distributed them to the kids. "Don't let 'em catch fire—then they'll be all charred."

Poppy smiled at Mitchell, feeling calm now that he was here. He'd always done that, made her comfortable. Right now that was what she needed: comfort.

He arched an eyebrow at her and grinned.

"He's a handsome man," Rose whispered. "A girl could do much worse."

Poppy nodded. There was no arguing the truth. Mitchell was a good man. Handsome to boot. But Mitchell didn't set her on fire. He didn't make her world tip, her insides melt and her lungs ache for air. His touch didn't make every inch of her tighten and yearn. Only one man did that. She stared into the leaping flames, pushing the image of Toben Boone aside.

"Want one?" Rowdy asked, offering her a marshmallow.

Seconds later chocolate and marshmallow covered all three kids' cheeks and chins.

"Now, that's a picture." Bob laughed. "Y'all squish together and say cheese."

The kids did, hamming it up with silly faces.

"How's the road been treating you?" Rose asked Mitchell.

"Good, good. No complaints. I'm lucky, doing something I love and getting to see a little bit of the world, too." His rich voice rolled over them.

Poppy grinned, knowing he was "on" for her sister and brother-in-law. She could always tell because his emcee voice took over. She shook her head, popping the last of her s'more into her mouth.

"No thoughts of settling down someplace?" Rose asked.

Mitchell shrugged. "From time to time. But I figure I've got to take the hand I've been dealt and play it through."

Poppy rolled her eyes, shooting him a look. *Really?*

Rose pushed. "No special lady? You don't want a family?"

"Rose." Bob sighed. "Another s'more?"

Rose shook her head, holding up her hand to ward off the s'more Bob was offering up. "Excuse me for caring. Mitchell's been a part of our family for…years. I can't help wanting to see him settled and happy."

Mitchell shot Poppy a look. They both knew what her sister was up to. Rose had been devastated when they called off their engagement. More devastated than either of them. If they ever thought to try again, Poppy had no doubt that Rose would be over the moon.

Headlights bounced along her driveway, and Poppy stood to see better. It was too dark to be sure, but the truck was white and she thought she could see the Boone Ranch logo on its door.

Toben? Now?

She glanced back at her sister, then Mitchell.

"Who is that?" Bob asked.

"Probably someone who's all turned around," Poppy murmured.

"I'll set 'em straight," Mitchell offered, heading toward the truck before Poppy could stop him.

Poppy glanced at Rowdy, happily stacking far too much chocolate onto a new s'more. She'd let Mitchell handle it. A talk with Toben needed to happen, but right now wasn't the time. She was still angry from his sudden absence—and Rowdy's distress. She would only get worked up. Rose would pick up on that and turn it into something big and dramatic.

"Want another one?" Rowdy asked, offering her the overflowing s'more.

"That's not going to fit into a human's mouth," Poppy argued. "Not without the need for a bath and scrubbing afterward."

"I don't mind," Rowdy said, shoving a third of the sticky sandwich into his mouth.

Bob glanced over his shoulder in the direction Mitchell had gone. "You're sort of isolated out here, aren't you?" he asked.

Poppy smiled. "One of the perks of living in the country."

"You should get a big dog," Bob suggested. "Or two."

"Or a husband," Rose murmured.

"Can we, Ma?" Rowdy asked. "I want a dog."

"You've already got Cheeto to take care of. You don't think a dog would be one more thing?" She used her bandanna to try to remove some of the chocolate from his cheek.

"Cheeto's the best but I'm not sure he'd let us know if a stranger was snooping around." Rowdy licked off the tips of his fingers.

"That's true, Aunt Poppy," Dot agreed.

"Get a big, mean dog," Otis added. "Something scary."

Poppy laughed. "I'm not sure I want a big, mean, scary dog around the place. But maybe I'll think about getting a dog."

"Or a husband." Rose smiled, taking a cautious bite off her s'more.

"Look who I found." Mitchell's voice was off. She glanced back to see Toben at his side.

"Dad!" Rowdy jumped up, forgetting how sticky he was as he launched himself for a hug.

Toben caught him, hugging him tight. "Looks like there's a party going on."

Poppy stood, hating the nervousness that washed over her. She should be happy he was here, for Rowdy. But damn if his brief absence didn't reinforce her original reservations about welcoming Toben into their lives. No matter how much she wanted to believe he'd change for Rowdy, that he'd stay and be a father, she wouldn't. Worse, she feared her hope, her belief in him, would only end up hurting them.

Mitchell came to her side, his hand resting on her shoulder—squeezing lightly. "He wouldn't leave," he whispered.

Poppy nodded, patting his hand.

"Oops, sorry," Rowdy said, assessing the chocolate-and-marshmallow smear he'd left on Toben's gray T-shirt.

"It's fine." Toben looked at the mess. "Be even better

if there's more. To eat. Not to wear." His gaze found hers, his smile hardening as his gaze traveled to her shoulder— and Mitchell's hand.

"I'll make you one," Otis volunteered.

"Extra chocolate?" Rowdy asked.

"Sure." Toben nodded at Bob. "Toben Boone."

Bob's laugh was startled. "I figured as much. Bob Mills." He shook hands with Toben. "This is my wife, Rose."

"Poppy's sister." Toben's megawatt smile was hard to refuse. "It's nice to meet you. You've got great kids."

Rose nodded, her expression bewildered. "Thank you."

"Here, Dad." Rowdy patted the stump next to him. "Almost ready."

Toben moved, sitting beside Rowdy. "What have you been up to?"

"We worked in Ma's shop," Rowdy said. "Painted the bathroom and break room. Helped put the new belt buckles and boleros in the display case—after we cleaned all the glass. There's a lot of glass in that place."

Poppy smiled. The three of them had worked hard, with few complaints. "The place is really coming together. Thanks to the three of you."

"Sounds like she's working you all pretty hard. How's the pay?" Mitchell asked.

"Ice cream." Otis smiled.

"And pie," Rowdy added.

"Sounds like a fair working wage to me," Toben said.

"What do you do, Mr. Boone?" Rose asked.

"He's a cowboy." Rowdy's matter-of-fact delivery made Toben smile.

"I work on the family ranch, ma'am." Toben took the s'more Rowdy offered him.

"No more rodeo days for you?" Rose asked, her tone

snippy. "Poppy said there was nothing more important to you than the rodeo."

Toben looked at her. "That was true, once. But not anymore."

"How long has it been since you were on the circuit?" Mitchell asked, sitting down on the log, prompting Poppy to do so, as well. "Couple of years now?"

Toben nodded.

"And in that time you've been working on your family's ranch?" Rose asked.

Toben nodded again.

"Does this work provide a decent income?"

Poppy stared at her sister.

"What?" Rose refused to back down. "He has a son, responsibilities. I'm Rowdy's aunt—I care about him. And you." She took Poppy's hand in hers.

"And while I appreciate that, this isn't the time or the place." Poppy leveled a stare at her sister. Her sister's lack of understanding about boundaries was stepping on her last nerve.

"You don't have to worry, Mom," Otis said. "Toben wants Rowdy now."

The only sound was the pop of the burning wood and the rhythmic chirp of the crickets.

Poppy didn't know who she was more irritated with: Rose or Toben. Otis was a kid—he thought he was reassuring his mother. When all he'd done was remind everyone what was really going on. Not that she had a clear understanding of what, exactly, was going on. She sighed. Why hadn't Toben just left? She knew Mitchell would have been as persuasive as possible—so why resist? It could have been a perfectly nice evening if he'd just driven away.

"We need more graham crackers." She needed space to collect herself.

"I'll get them," Mitchell offered.

"No." She stood, shot him a tight smile and headed into the house.

Poppy hurried to her bathroom and washed her face and hands, running cold water along the back of her neck. She paced the room twice, drawing in long, deep breaths. Why was she so agitated? Her sister was a pain in the ass, but that was nothing new. And this time, she was trying to put Rowdy's best interests first. Poppy understood—part of her shared the same worries.

And Toben? Learning to control her reaction to him was a necessary survival skill. He wasn't stupid; he was aware she wasn't immune to him. Hopefully, he didn't realize the extent to which she ached for him—wildly, dangerously... But she didn't like it. Worse, she didn't know how to stop. Even now, though she was frustrated and angry with him, the pull of heat between them was there.

She headed back down the hall to the kitchen, her steps slowing when she saw Toben was waiting for her. "I need a minute—"

"I know." But he stood there—looking far too tempting. His gray shirt hugged his broad shoulders and clung to the well-muscled contours of his chest. "I'm sorry."

His apology was a surprise. She crossed her arms over her chest, holding herself tightly. He did look sorry. "For what?" A blanket apology wasn't going to cut it, not this time. She wasn't about to make this easy on him.

He stepped forward. "Where do I start?" He frowned, a deep crease forming between his brows.

She swallowed, his heat rolling over her and weakening

her resolve. "Now's not the time, Toben. And I'm not the one you need to apologize to."

"No?" he asked, closing the gap between them. "I think we've wasted enough time. I'm sorry for being a selfish sonofabitch. I'm sorry you had to raise Rowdy on your own. I'm sorry you thought I didn't want him…or you. Because I do, every damn day."

"Every day?" Her expression was surprised. She was not going to let his words make her feel warm and fuzzy. Nope. No way. "Even the last three days? Toben, you should have been here. Or called."

"You're right—I should have," he agreed.

But she wasn't done. "The last few days Rowdy's wondered what he did to send you away. He asked me if it was because he hadn't gone to dinner with the Boones, that maybe his cousins were right about you changing your mind." She let her anger swallow the tingles his closeness stirred. "I won't lie for you, Toben. I don't lie."

"I know." His voice was raw, his expression devastated.

"I didn't know what to say to him. You can't just show up when you want, like now, then leave him with no word. He's a boy, a child. Children need reassurance and consistency and routine. Maybe…maybe we should talk to a lawyer about a formal custody—"

"Poppy?" Mitchell's voice, Mitchell's booted steps on the wooden porch.

Poppy edged around Toben, but his hand caught her arm.

"I won't let him down again," Toben said. "I promise you that."

His blue gaze locked with hers, searching for something… His hand was warm, his thumb featherlight on her skin. Too simple a touch to leave her breathless.

Poppy tugged free—but she knew Mitchell had seen the

awkward exchange. She didn't look at Mitchell until the back door had swung shut, signaling Toben's departure. If Mitchell was smart, he'd keep his comments to himself.

"Needing help finding those graham crackers?" Mitchell asked.

She glared at him.

He chuckled. "He gets under your skin something fierce."

She continued to glare at him.

"Is that what you want?" Mitchell asked. "All that fire?"

"Toben?" she asked, taking the box of graham crackers out of the pantry.

Mitchell raised a brow. "Hard to miss. You two were talking about something important."

"Rowdy... That's all." She paused, shaking her head and speaking with a little more emphasis. "What else—"

"Looks like there's more going on." Mitchell's gaze never wavered. "Like you two might be working out the kinks in your relationship."

"There's no relationship," she murmured. How the hell did she define what they had? They'd had a child together. Was there a label for that? Her irritation ratcheted up.

"Good." Mitchell's hand covered hers. "Because he gets you all in a frenzy. I worry once that fire's gone, he will be, too."

Poppy dropped the box of graham crackers, hearing her own concerns voiced aloud.

"We're best friends," he continued. "I love Rowdy like my own. We, you and me, understand each other. You want to give Rowdy a steady, good life. Make sure you know he can give that to you before you let things go too far. Okay?" Mitchell's gaze searched hers.

Poppy smiled, then nodded. He was right. She knew he was right.

"Where are the graham crackers?" Rowdy asked, slamming into the kitchen with Otis following.

"Here," Mitchell said. "Your ma dropped the box, so they might be broken." He winked at her. She rolled her eyes in answer.

"Ma." Rowdy sighed.

"Harder to make s'mores like that," Otis agreed.

"Bet we can figure it out." Mitchell steered them to the back door.

Poppy let them go, holding on to the kitchen counter as her emotions swung from one end of the spectrum to the other. As attracted as she might be to Toben, she knew there was no future with him—not romantically. She wasn't willing to risk her heart on him. No, Toben's only interest was being there for Rowdy.

She blew out a deep breath and stared out the screen door.

If she had it her way, she'd kick them all out, bar the gate and enjoy some peace and quiet—just her, Rowdy and the horses.

TOBEN PROMISED ROWDY a ride on Boone Ranch—after his aunt and uncle left. Nothing like receiving icy looks and veiled insults to make a fella feel at home. The fact that Mitchell wore a smug grin most of the evening made it worse. Yes, the family liked the guy. Yes, he had history with Rowdy and Poppy that Toben would never have. He knew better than to start something with the man, but it was hard not to take the bait.

The only consolation he had was Poppy. It was plain to see she considered Mitchell a friend—that was all.

The exact opposite of the way she reacted to Toben. Tensing up, trying to keep distance between them or wrapping her arms around her waist, like she was holding back. From reaching for him? As much as he wanted to kiss her until she was breathless and soft in his arms, he didn't want to scare her off. If something were to happen between them, he'd make damn sure there was no ambivalence on her part. Their night together had been her idea, on her terms. He suspected those terms—one night of no-holds-barred bedroom fun—wouldn't satisfy him anymore. It wasn't just his body that ached for her. Until he knew what that meant, he wasn't going off half-cocked.

Monday was long. He sent a few pics to Rowdy on Poppy's phone, but he didn't get a response. By late afternoon, he was restless. He and Deacon headed into town for some pool at Cutter's bar. The crowd and noise might be just the right distraction for him.

"Beer?" Deacon asked, heading toward the bar.

Toben nodded, making his way to the pool tables. His gaze swept the room. Mostly familiar faces. A few sunburned tourists and wannabe cowboys, too. With the Fourth coming up, the town would be full of freshly purchased ill-fitting cowboy hats and boots that had never seen real work or dust. Toben grinned at two female tourists who were whispering and giggling, staring openly him. He wasn't one to shy away from attention. If tipping his hat made their night, he'd do it. Might just throw in a wink for good measure.

"Next you'll be buying them a drink." Poppy's voice startled him, drawing his attention around the pool table. She stood, pool cue in hand. "What was it you'd say? 'I was looking for you'? or 'Were you looking for me?' Or was it 'I found you'? It worked, normally." She shook her head. "Old habits die hard, I guess."

Toben felt heat in his cheeks. "I never said, 'I found

you,'" he argued, but she remembered the others? Course, she'd been front row center for more than a few of his conquests. And each time she'd been sitting there, rolling her eyes and shaking her head at him, he'd gone home alone—amused. "I was smiling, Poppy, being a cowboy they can remember fondly."

"Smiling, huh?" she asked, rubbing the cue tip in chalk. "I've seen where your smiles lead."

Damn straight she had. Not that it had worked on her. Not until she'd turned the tables on him. That night was the best night of his life—and the worst morning. He cleared his throat, turning all his charm on her. He loved the way her eyes widened, then narrowed. She wasn't as immune to him as she wanted to be. "No harm ever came from smiling at a pretty lady, Poppy White."

Poppy's brows rose. "I guess that depends on how you define *harm*."

"Rowdy here?" he asked, his gaze sweeping the room.

"In a bar?" she asked, her brows ever higher.

"It's not that kind of place. No hard liquor, just beer. On weekends there's dancing in the back. Families come." He could just imagine Rowdy running around, making friends and learning to dance. "Rowdy know how to two-step?"

Poppy nodded. "A little. Not much time for dancing."

"That's a shame. You should always make time for dancing." He grinned. "But seriously, you're raising that boy right."

Her expression changed, softening beneath his praise. He liked her full of fight, but her sweetness was a thing to see. All rosy cheeks, wide eyes and a hesitant smile.

"Speaking of dancing." He nodded through the doors. "How about it?"

That snapped her out of it. "No."

"Feeling rusty?" He nodded, sighing. "Guess I should thank you for saving my toes."

"It's not going to work." She rolled her eyes.

"What?" he teased, his smile growing.

"I'm not going to dance with you. Besides, can't imagine your date would appreciate it." Her brown gaze darted around.

"That's considerate. But I'm pretty sure my cousin won't mind." He pointed at Deacon, resting his elbows on the counter and staring at the television. Clips of bull rides were playing. "Looks like I'll be waiting on my beer. Might as well dance with me, pass the time."

She grinned. "Nope."

"Your date mind?" he asked.

"He might." Her gaze locked with his.

Dammit. "Where is Mitchell, the good man?" He couldn't keep the sneer out of his voice.

"He got a call," she said, nodding at the window.

Toben turned. There he was, cell phone to his ear, slowly walking back and forth on the porch. "He going back on the road?" he asked.

"Maybe."

Her tone pulled him back to her. She looked…confused. A little sad, maybe. He didn't like it. "How about we go one round. I win, you dance with me."

Her eyes slammed into his, her grin instantaneous. "What do I get if I win?"

He swallowed back the offer that sprang to his lips. Whatever she wanted, he'd give it to her. Did she know how much she got to him? That standing here so close, her scent pulled at him, willing him to step closer—and touch her. "What does a woman like you want, Poppy White?"

Her brows, and her temper, were up again. "A woman like me? Meaning?"

He stepped closer, letting his arm brush against her as he reached for a pool cue. He felt her shiver. Hell, he shivered, too. Touching her was like touching fire. Fluid, electric, alive. His voice was rough when he spoke. "Strong. Independent. Smart. Determined." He stared down at her. "Beautiful. Sexy."

Her lips parted, her flush deepening.

"All good things," he finished. "An original."

She blinked, tearing her gaze from his and circling the pool table. "Rack 'em up. Or do you want me to?"

He chuckled and placed the pool balls into the break, centered them and stepped back. "Ladies first."

Her smile was impish, and fifteen minutes later, he knew why. She'd beaten him without giving him a single shot. "I figured out a few ways to earn money on the circuit," she explained.

He held up his hands in defeat. "That was impressive."

She kept on smiling. "It was, wasn't it?"

"So what do you want?" he asked. "You won, fair and square."

Her gaze fell to his lips, lingering just long enough to have him shifting in his starched jeans. "I'll let you know." She put the pool cue back on the rack.

"She just handed you your ass." Deacon arrived, handing his longneck to Poppy. "So she deserves the beer. Deacon Boone. Glad to meet a woman who can knock this cocky son of a gun down a peg."

Poppy took the beer, laughing. "I'm not going to lie. It's nice."

Deacon nodded. "I take it you know him?"

She shrugged. "Sort of. Used to, anyway. I'd sit in the corner and watch him. I don't know what was more disappointing—that he went home with someone warm and willing nine times out of ten…or that so many women are so damn gullible."

"I like her," Deacon said. "What'd you do to lose this one?"

"What can I say, I'm an idiot." Toben shook his head. "Remember it all too well."

She snorted. "Right. I broke your heart. It took you a whole…week before you were out trawling again."

Toben stared at her, remembering just how quick he was to stumble into every bar—hoping she'd be there. When she wasn't, he'd drink until he could almost believe the woman he took back to his hotel room was enough. And every damn morning, he'd wake up wishing Poppy were next to him so he could beg her to stay. "I'm not sure my heart ever got over you, Poppy."

"You're Poppy?" Deacon groaned.

But Poppy was studying him.

"It took him six months to sober up. Damn hard work, dragging his passed-out ass from hotel room to hotel room so he could sleep it off." Deacon paused. "Guess you weren't doing much drinking, though. Where's the boy? Rowdy?"

"He's home with his aunt and uncle," Poppy said, her gaze staying fixed on Toben. "They're leaving in the morning."

"Nice of them. Considering you've had Otis and Dot for…?" Toben asked. Her brother-in-law seemed okay. The sister, he wasn't sure about.

"A couple of weeks," Poppy answered. "It's going to be awfully quiet once they're gone." But she didn't look disappointed.

"When's Mitchell headed out?" he asked, studying her right back.

"No idea," she answered, her attention shifting to the window.

His gaze followed, but Mitchell wasn't there. He was

inside, carrying two longnecks toward the pool table. He nodded at Toben and Deacon, apparently not the least bit bothered by their presence. So why the hell did Mitchell being here bother Toben so much?

"Beer?" he asked, holding the longneck out to her.

"It's his," she said, pointing at Toben. "I won his in pool."

"That's not what you won," Toben argued.

"She's a pool shark," Mitchell said. "What did you win?"

Poppy took a long swig of her beer, looking between him and Mitchell. She chuckled. "I don't know yet."

"Lady's choice," Toben offered, enjoying the instant tightening of Mitchell's jaw far too much.

Chapter Twelve

"Anything else over here, Ma?" Rowdy called to her.

Poppy dug through the packing paper, pulling out the last trophy. Her dad's. The gold had been all but rubbed off the plastic cup, and the metal nameplate was slipping on the marble base, but it was a treasure. She smiled, running her finger over her father's name. Barron White. Calf Scramble Champion, Gillespie County Fair. "Your grandpa's trophy," she answered, carrying it from the break room.

Rowdy waited, arranging memorabilia on the wooden shelf that ran around the top of the shop. Her entire family's career was on display, including some of her mother's handiwork. She'd been a master seamstress and quilter. Poppy had mounted the christening gown her mother had pieced, smocked and embroidered by hand in an oblong case.

Most of the pictures she displayed were copies, the originals showcased back at the house. Wherever she was, she liked to have her family around her. The quilts that covered every bed in the house and filled her large wood chest were made by her mother and grandmother. Cuddling up beneath them was as close to a hug as she could get. "Am I old enough to try the calf scramble this year?" Rowdy asked, placing the trophy on the shelf.

"Not yet. The youngest I've seen is ten. But we'll check and see, okay? Safety first." She wasn't worried about

Rowdy's behavior, but some of the older boys could get a little competitive in the arena. He was big for six, but the cutoff for a calf scramble was seventeen. And while she knew being rough-and-tumble was part of being a cowboy, she wasn't sure she was ready to see her boy knocked around—or his confidence dinged.

"I know, Ma." But his sigh said it all. He was disappointed. "How's it look?"

She stepped back. "Maybe a little to the left?" She nodded when he moved it. "Perfect. Just enough room to put a few of yours up there."

"What about Dad?" Rowdy asked, climbing down the ladder. "Think he'd want to put any of his stuff up here? Since he's family and all?"

Poppy smiled at her son, hiding the conflict his words stirred. Toben was Rowdy's father, not necessarily her family. And yet she understood his desire to include him. To Rowdy, Toben's addition was a gift. For her... Well, she still wasn't sure what he was to her—beyond exasperating. "You can ask him."

"Okay." Rowdy nodded. He sat, looking around the shop. "The place looks good, Ma. Real good."

Poppy looked around the shop as well, excited to see her vision coming to life. This was real. And, if she did say so herself, awesome. Every nook and cranny just as she'd imagined—neat, tidy and inviting to shoppers. Not just tourists, mind you, but hardworking ranching and rodeo folk, too.

The left of the shop was all fashion—men's and women's. Everything from boots to hats, silly socks to cowboy-print pajamas, ladies' blinged-out jeans, jewelry, Wranglers, work wear, his-and-hers pearl-snap button-downs and some fancier rodeo-worthy attire.

The right side of the shop was housewares, rodeo gear,

and saddle and tack supplies. The smell of leather and wood polish scented the air. She'd stocked harnesses, saddle pads, stirrups and a sample book of fabric for saddle pads. She had little figurines made from discarded horseshoes, painted plaques, cowboy joke books and a wide array of cookbooks and kitchenware.

All surrounded by rodeo posters, memorabilia and bits and pieces of her family's history.

"Yep," she said, hands on hips, nodding. "Almost ready, don't you think?"

The door opened, admitting Renata Boone. "Am I intruding?" she asked, her attention lingering on Rowdy.

So she knew about Rowdy. Did all the Boones know he was one of them? "No, come on in," Poppy said, smiling. "We were just putting up a few things."

"I love what you've done with the shop, Poppy. We've got the one hat and boot shop, but they don't have the selection you've got." Renata spun slowly around, then poked and explored several shelves. "This is adorable." She smiled. "When are you opening?"

"I thought Fourth of July weekend made the most sense."

She nodded. "That's a great idea. I know the Shops Association would love to throw a grand opening celebration for you, invite your shop neighbors and friends. Maybe a day or two before?" She paused. "Good way to meet everyone on Main Street."

"Thank you—that sounds wonderful, Renata." Poppy was stunned by the offer.

"Well, it is part of my job." Renata grinned. "But I'm really excited you've picked Stonewall Crossing to call home. But I do have a favor to ask. We'd love for you to ride in the Grand Entry, carry the American flag. If you're interested?"

Poppy's side ached just thinking about balancing the heavy flagpole while riding.

"Will you, Ma?" Rowdy asked. "Stormy would love that."

"You want me to?" she asked, his answer written all over his face.

"You don't have to let me know right away." Renata smiled at Rowdy. "You planning on rodeoing?"

Rowdy shrugged, standing a little straighter as he admitted, "I've won a couple of belt buckles mutton-busting."

"Sounds like you've already started." Renata held her hand out. "Like your mom and your dad. Toben's my cousin, so that makes us cousins, too. We haven't officially met. I'm Renata Boone."

"Hi." Poppy saw his eyes go wide, a smile on his face. "You're a lot nicer than my other cousins," he said, shaking her hand. "It's a real pleasure to meet you."

Renata laughed. "You, too, Rowdy. Toben's always talking about you."

His smile grew ever bigger.

Poppy nudged her boy. "You can tell Rowdy's not at all pleased to hear that." She did her best to shove aside the constant doubt his excitement caused.

"I'm really glad you decided to settle here," Renata said. "The Boones are going to welcome you with wide-open arms. Fair warning, there's a passel of us. And we're all about family."

"That's all right. Me and Ma won't be lonely now." Rowdy nudged his mother back, all dimples and bright eyes.

Her heart thumped.

"You'll have that," Renata assured him. "And then some. Hope you'll come to the next family get-together? The both of you?"

Poppy stared at the woman. Her blue eyes waited, no hint of teasing or judgment clouding her pretty face. The woman was serious...and it made Poppy think. Just because Toben might not stick around didn't mean his fam-

ily would bail on Rowdy. For the first time, Poppy saw the
Boones as potential allies for her son—people who would
be there for him regardless of his father's actions. And she
was overwhelmingly relieved by that possibility.

"He tried to bring us before," Rowdy said, his cheeks
flaming red. "But I chickened out."

Renata nodded. "Understandable. Just know we're
not strangers—we're family, so there's nothing to worry
over." She smiled at Poppy. "One thing I love about being
a Boone—we've got each other's backs, through thick and
thin." Renata wasn't just talking to her son. "I should be
heading out. It's been a long day and I'm stopping off to
visit Tandy on my way home. Have you met Tandy yet?
She's Toben's twin sister."

"Dad has a twin?" Rowdy asked.

"Guess that's a no. Your aunt is one of the sweetest gals
ever, a real brain, too. She's studying to be a veterinarian
over at the university. I bet she'd love to take you on a tour,
show you all the animals. She's going to be tickled pink to
meet you." Renata touched his cheek.

Rowdy nodded. "I'd like that. Ma and I are thinking
about getting us a dog or two."

Poppy laughed. "Oh, we are?"

Rowdy's grin was triumphant. "A boy needs a dog, Ma.
And you should have one, too, so they don't get lonely when
we're not home."

"Or they could come to the shop," Renata said. "The ladies at the hair salon have a few cats that sit in the custom-
ers' laps while they're getting their hair done. It's a hoot."

"Huh?" Rowdy shook his head. "A cat's fine, I guess,
but I think we need dogs."

"I'll keep my ears open for you," Renata offered.

Poppy knew they'd end up with a dog or two before
the summer was out. Now that it was just her and Rowdy,

he was bound to get lonely. And, as he pointed out, a boy should have a dog. As long as Cheeto didn't mind too much.

"I'm off," Renata said.

"It was nice chatting with you, Renata," Poppy said, meaning it.

"You, too." The woman waved and turned, then stopped. "Oh, wait, I almost forgot. We have a big scavenger hunt out on the ranch on Fourth of July weekend, too—a fundraiser for the refuge my brother Archer runs. On horseback, of course. You and Rowdy could form a team, if you want, or join one."

Rowdy stared up at her. "That sounds like fun."

"It does," Poppy agreed. "How do we sign up?"

"I'll give Toben a registration form and have him bring it out to you."

Poppy nodded. "Sounds good."

"I'll be in touch." She opened the door. "It was nice to meet you, Rowdy."

"Bye," Rowdy called out, turning a huge smile Poppy's way once they were alone. "Maybe Dad will be on a team with us—for the scavenger hunt? Think he will, Ma?"

"Only way to find out is to ask him." She ruffled Rowdy's hair. She glanced at the large windmill-shaped clock that hung on the back wall. It was almost four. "How about a swim?"

She and Rowdy had given Rose and Bob a tour of the place before her sister's family left. She and Rose hadn't been close in a long time but it had been hard saying goodbye to Dot and Otis. The four of them had started getting along so well—having fun and making memories she hoped they'd treasure as they grew. She and Bob made sure dates for next year were set, making the goodbyes a little easier. Rose, as impressed with the shop as she'd been with the house, had been eager to hustle the kids into their SUV and hit the road. Poppy and Rowdy stood waving until the car had turned off Main Street, then stuck around to add some finishing touches to the two changing stalls and put up the last of the decorations. Her boy deserved some fun.

Rowdy jumped up. "Sounds great."

Poppy grinned, walking through the shop and turning off lights before locking up behind them. After having Dot and Otis with them, she hoped Rowdy was enjoying the quiet as much as she was. She knew it was a more isolated existence for him—for her, too. On the circuit, there'd always been people to talk to and things to do and see.

"You happy, Rowdy?" she asked, meeting his gaze in the rearview mirror.

"Yes, ma'am," he answered, grinning. "Only thing that could make me happier is a dog."

TOBEN PARKED THE TRUCK, waved at Rowdy and tried not to react to how pretty Poppy looked. His son was dripping wet, the inner tube under his arm almost as big as he was. Poppy was wrapped in a towel, the straps of her bikini top displaying the golden skin beneath. He sucked in a deep breath, steadying himself. Tonight was about the three of them growing closer as a family. Not him getting waylaid by his want for her. He opened the truck door and slid out, grabbing the bag of groceries he'd brought. "Hope you're hungry," he said.

"Starved." Rowdy was all smiles. "Need help?"

"Sure." Toben grinned at his son. "Poppy."

She nodded. "Toben."

"Sure is quiet," he said, following Rowdy into the kitchen.

"It's nice, isn't it?" Rowdy asked. "Aunt Rose and Uncle Bob left this morning."

"Come on, Rowdy, be nice. I think your cousins were sad to go." Poppy pulled the door shut behind them.

"I guess. But it was time, Ma." Rowdy shrugged.

Poppy shook her head. "You go change before you make a puddle on the floor. Then you can help your dad."

"Yes, ma'am." Rowdy ran down the hall.

Toben watched his son go, pleased with his willing attitude. A nice change from Poppy's niece and nephew. He glanced at Poppy, then away—the sight of her too great a temptation. Best to say something to distract himself until he could forget that she was wearing next to nothing— even wrapped in a towel—standing within arm's reach. He cleared his throat. "You're missing Otis and Dot?" Toben asked, pulling the food from the brown paper sack.

She didn't answer, so he looked at her.

She grinned, wrinkled her nose and shook her head. "Not really," she whispered, sounding guilty.

He laughed. "That's okay."

"Rowdy and I haven't really had time to make this place our own yet. To settle in, just the two of us. It's all still pretty new." She tugged her towel tighter, taking in the room with assessing eyes. "Once those new appliances get here, I'll be downright happy."

He wasn't going to let her "just the two of us" comment get to him. Not tonight. He was going to put in the work to show her it didn't need to be just the two of them...and hope she'd come around to his way of thinking. Toben's gaze fell to her exposed shoulder. "When will that be?"

"Soon, I hope." She looked at him, then away. "What do you need? For dinner?"

"A bowl. And something to marinate the chicken in. Otherwise, I think I got it covered." He pulled out the fresh green beans. "Rowdy ever snapped beans?"

Poppy took the bag. "It's time he learned. I'm hoping to put in a garden."

"Soil's good for it," he agreed.

"I need to read up on what grows best here, but I'm hoping beans, tomatoes, potatoes, corn, some squash... Guess I'm rambling." She broke off.

He glanced at her, shaking the bottle of his uncle's homemade barbecue sauce. "Are you?" He liked listening to her talk, and knowing she had plans for this place made him...happy.

"You want to hear me talking about my gardening plans?" she asked, rolling her eyes.

"Why not?" he asked. "Uncle Teddy has a big garden. Well, it was Aunt Mag's. When she passed, we all sort of pitched in to keep it going. Now a couple of the people that work at the Lodge—the bed-and-breakfast on the ranch—have taken over. It's impressive, all sorts of vegetables and herbs. It's where I got some of our dinner." He looked at her. "I'll show you when you come out."

She put the beans on the counter. "Renata stopped by the shop today."

He grinned. "And?"

"She says you have a sister?" She paused. "A twin?"

His grin grew. "I do. I haven't told you about Tandy? Still not sure if I'm coming or going."

"I... There's still a lot we don't know about each other," she said.

He looked at her, nodding. "I'm hoping we can change that?"

Her brown eyes were intense, searching his face. "I'd like that." She blew out a slow breath, her voice high and tight. "For Rowdy."

"What about me?" Rowdy asked. "You gonna change, Ma?"

"I'm going." Poppy nodded. "I'll be back."

"Were you talking about getting me a dog?" Rowdy asked.

She laughed. "No, we were *not* talking about getting you a dog." She shook her head, walking down the hallway to her room.

"You want a dog?" Toben asked.

"Uncle Bob said we were awful far away from town, with no alarm or protection." Rowdy shrugged. "A dog would fix that. Or two."

Toben nodded, not liking the truth in Bob's words. They were alone, a good fifteen minutes from town. Almost forty minutes from Boone Ranch. Pretty damn isolated for a woman and small boy. Not that Poppy couldn't handle things—she could. But...a dog was a good idea. And soon. "It would. Your ma's not keen on the idea?"

"Not yet." Rowdy poked the bag. "Green beans?"

"Not a fan?" Toben asked, chuckling at the face his son made.

The boy shook his head.

"That's okay." Toben bent and whispered, "I've got a secret way to make them taste good."

Rowdy didn't believe him. "Green beans? Taste good?"

Toben chuckled again. "Yes sirree. I'll show you how to snap off the ends first."

Five minutes later, Rowdy was at the table, throwing the snapped beans in a colander and the ends in a bag. While Rowdy was working on the beans, Toben started boiling macaroni and chopped up some bacon and onions to sauté.

"You cook?" Poppy asked, returning to the kitchen in jeans and a pink T-shirt hugging all-too-perfect curves. Her hair was loose and wet, thick curls hanging down her back.

He shrugged. "A bit."

"Can I help?" she asked.

He shook his head. "Clara sent another pie for dessert. Apple this time."

"I thought I smelled cinnamon," Poppy said, peering into the bag before pulling the dessert out.

"Who's Clara?" Rowdy asked, still snapping away.

"My uncle Teddy's new wife," Toben said. "His first wife, Aunt Mags, died a while back. We all thought Uncle Teddy was done with romance, but Clara showed up and he was all flowers and valentines."

"You like her?" Rowdy asked.

"I do." Toben tossed the bacon and onions in the skillet. "Only person in my family I don't always see eye to eye with is my cousin Archer. But he's a mite better now that he's married. Eden, his wife, and his two little girls seem to have taken some of the...starch out of him."

"Starch?" Rowdy asked.

Toben glanced at Poppy, who was grinning. "He's sort of...uptight. A know-it-all. A little...rough around the edges. But he's better, for the most part."

Toben had arrived with no expectations for their evening. He hoped it would go well. He hoped he'd drive away feeling like he and his son were growing closer—that Poppy was settling into this new arrangement. But laughing, sharing stories, working in the kitchen together, was so much more. Dinner was good, made better by the company. It was new and fragile, but there was a sense of family here. He wanted to protect it and watch it grow.

"Huh," Rowdy said, between bites.

Toben couldn't help but notice his son's plate was almost empty. Green beans included. "Huh?" he repeated.

"They were good." Rowdy winked.

"Bacon does that." Toben winked back.

Poppy laughed. "I'll start washing up. Since you cooked."

But Toben couldn't sit still. He helped clear off the table and took the trash out, returning to find the pie cut and on plates. Rowdy had a million questions about the scavenger hunt and the Fourth of July festivities.

"I've only been here for a couple of years—on the rodeo circuit long while before that," Toben confessed. "My mother lives in Montana."

"Miss her?" Rowdy asked.

Toben was aware that both Poppy and Rowdy were waiting for an answer. He sat his fork down, a small smile on his face. "Well, now, Rowdy. I'd like to say I'm as close to my mother as you are, but that's not the case."

"Because she won't tell you who your dad is?" Rowdy asked, causing Poppy to cough and choke.

Toben patted her on the back while Rowdy got her a glass of water. She stared at him, her eyes wide over the rim of her glass.

"That's part of it," Toben agreed, not wanting to ruin the tone of their evening. Poppy was still staring at him. What he wouldn't give to know what she was thinking.

Rowdy nodded. "I like apple pie."

"Me, too," he agreed. "All of Clara's pies are good." Which was true. And one of the reasons his uncle was getting a little belly on him. "After work sometime, how about we go to the veterinary hospital? You can meet my sister and see if there are any dogs looking for a home."

"Really?" Rowdy asked.

"Really." Toben nodded. Until he met Poppy's eyes. She wasn't happy. Dammit. "Maybe... I guess... You know a dog's a lot of work?"

Rowdy nodded. "Yes, sir. So is Cheeto. And I keep him happy." He looked at his mother. "Don't I, Ma?"

Poppy nodded. "You do."

Toben knew he'd messed up. Through the game of dominoes, she kept her eyes averted. She agreed to let him put Rowdy to bed without a single word. And when he walked down the hall, he felt the hostility rolling off her in waves. Best to start off with an apology and hope for the best. "I should have asked first—"

"Yes, you should have," she agreed, packing up the leftovers into the brown paper bag. "We're the adults, the two of us. We need to be on the same page when it comes to Rowdy. No more of…this. I don't know what you're going to say or do and it makes me…nervous." She spun around, her brown eyes flashing when they met his. "I'm trying… but you keep…you keep making things hard."

He frowned. He made her nervous? "I don't mean to."

"I know." Her tone rose. "I know you don't mean to. I know you want him to adore you. He does, believe me. You don't have to promise him dogs and big families. He'd be happy with just you, you know?"

His frustration sparked. "No, I don't know. I've never done this before. Ever. I'm learning as I go. All I know is I see him smile and I like it. I see him sad and it guts me."

Poppy blew out a slow breath, shaking her head.

"No dog?" he asked.

She made a little sound of irritation. "I can't tell him no now, can I? Then *I'm* the bad guy." A crease formed between her brows, her mouth pressing flat.

"I'm sorry, Poppy." He meant it. He ran a hand along the back of his neck. "Can't seem to get this right."

She opened her mouth, then closed it, made that angry little sound and crossed her arms over her chest. "Why did you fix the wall and stall in the barn?"

He shrugged.

"I was going to get to it." Her eyes flashed.

"I didn't mind," he said warily. Where was this going? Why the hell did a simple repair seem to be her tipping point?

"It's not your place." She shook her head. "You don't

need to do things for me, Toben. You don't need to cook dinner for me or…bring me flowers. You being here has nothing to do with me."

She didn't know how wrong she was. He wanted to do those things. He wanted to be a part of *her* daily life, not just Rowdy's. The more time he spent with her, the more he missed her when they were apart. But Ryder's warning had struck a nerve with him—being cautious was the right thing to do. She still thought of him as he had been, hell-bent on adventure and taking stupid risks. Maybe it was time to tell her he wasn't that man anymore and hope she'd give him a chance to prove it. "It bothers you?"

"Yes." The word was unsteady.

"Because you don't want my help? Or because I make you nervous?"

She stared at him, her cheeks flushing pink.

"Poppy?" He stepped forward, erasing the space between them. "I want to be a good man, too." He slid his arm around her waist. "It is about you." He pulled her against him. "It's about us." She felt so good, just being in his arms.

Her hands flexed against his chest, her voice wavering. "Don't you do that, Toben Boone. Don't you dare."

He froze, watching the fury on her face.

"Don't pretend you want me. That I'm special… Don't do that. Not now. I believed that before… But not this time. I can't be wild and crazy, Toben. I can't…give in to this and wake up to an empty bed." She stared at his chest, her hands fisting in the fabric of his shirt. "Don't make me want something that can't exist."

Her words sliced through his heart. She was special. *Special* wasn't enough. No, Poppy was the only woman who made him hope. Yes, he'd left her, acted like an ass and lost her. Until drinking had almost killed him. Even then, he'd look for her—hoping their paths would cross and he'd have another chance. This might not be how he'd envisioned it but he wasn't sorry. She was here, in his arms, resisting what they both wanted. Telling him she wanted him. Hell, not just wanted him, but wanted to be wild and crazy with him. His body was more than willing, but he didn't want to complicate things—not yet.

"Who said it can't exist? Dammit, Poppy, I want you," he ground out the words, unable to let her go. "So bad it hurts. But I—"

She kissed him then, her hands tangled in his hair and holding him tight. She was on tiptoe, swaying forward to melt against him. He groaned, his hold tightening on her, all but crushing her. Her scent wrapped around him as her lips moved against his, so soft.

She held on to him, hungry and desperate, the throb of her heart matching his own rapid beat. He should stop this before he was lost. As much as he ached for her, she didn't know how he felt. And loving her was more important than being in her bed.

But he'd forgotten how it was with her. How out of control they were together.

Her lips parted, the tip of her tongue teasing him. He groaned again, opening his mouth and welcoming the stroke of her tongue. His control crumpled then. Everything he needed was right here. No way he was letting her go. A shudder shook her as he deepened the kiss. His hand slid through her long curls and he cupped the back of her head to drink her in.

Her hands slid down, stroking the back of his neck before gripping his shoulders and pressing against him. Her touch rocked him to his core, kicking up both warning and an undeniable yearning. He paused, sucking in lungfuls of air, and stared at her. Her face was flushed, raw hunger in her dark eyes. His fingers traced along the curve of her cheek and jaw. She closed her eyes, turning into his touch—shivering as his thumb traced the edge of her full lips. She was beautiful, so damn beautiful. He couldn't resist.

A soft moan caught in the back of her throat as his lips traveled up the side of her neck to latch on to her earlobe. His teeth grazed the soft skin, the hitch in her breath stamping out any lingering restraint.

Her hands fell to his waist, tugging his shirt free. Her hands slid beneath the fabric, her fingers flexed against his spine, her nails lightly scoring up his back—covering his skin in goose bumps. When she tugged his T-shirt up and over his head, he ducked, eager to be rid of it. Anything that got him closer to her...

"Rowdy?" he asked, capturing her hands in his.

She blinked, her gaze falling from his. She was breathing heavy, the pulse in her throat thrumming rapidly. Her dark gaze held his as she took his hand and led him down the hall to her room. When they were inside, she pushed the door shut, facing him as she tugged her T-shirt over her head.

He didn't wait. His hands were gentle, sliding up her arms—savoring her soft, warm skin beneath his roughened touch. His fingers slid along the silken straps of her plain white silk bra, going round her back to free the clasp. He stepped closer, his eyes boring into hers, as the fabric fell away.

Their breathing was erratic, each gasp brushing her nipples against his chest. It was raw and electric, sweet and oh so tempting. His lips sought hers, his hands exploring her satin skin, sliding along her sides. He cupped the full weight of her breast, his thumb caressing the tip and driving them both mad.

One second she was in his arms, the next she was gone. He blinked, watching her strip, tossing her clothes without care. When she was naked, Toben could only stand and stare. She was more beautiful than he remembered, every curve and hollow demanding his attention.

"Damn, Poppy." His voice was low and husky.

Her smile wobbled.

He unbuttoned his jeans, then sat on the edge of the bed to tug his boots free. When his jeans and boxers hit the floor, Poppy pushed him back on the bed.

Toben rested on his elbows, watching her closely. She was inspecting him, sizing up the situation—he'd seen her do that on the circuit. Never rushing in without considering all the angles. He grinned. For all her show, she was nervous. Hell, he was nervous. And he was pretty sure he'd done this a hell of a lot more than she had.

He sat up, pulling her between his legs. His hands cupped her cheeks. She stared at him, swallowing, as he shook his head. "I found you," he whispered.

She kissed him, once, gently. Then again.

When her lips parted, his arms wrapped around her and pulled her beneath him. She gasped, her arms twining around his neck, her giggle soft. Damn but he loved the sound of it. Her hands gripped his back, her touch firm but unsteady.

No way he was going to rush this. Not until he'd tasted her. The tips of each breast. The sensitive skin along her sides. He paused, running a finger along several fine scars on her abdomen. He'd never noticed them before. But up close, they were impossible to miss. From her fall? He pressed kisses on each one. Her fingers tangled in his curls, but his hands and mouth weren't done. The curve of her hips. Her muscled calf. Behind her knee. His touch slid along her skin as he shifted between her thighs.

His gaze locked with hers as he eased slowly inside. Her lips parted and her nails bit into his back. Her heat engulfed him, tightly encasing him deep inside. It was incredible. She was incredible. He moved slowly, absorbing each shift and shudder of her body.

She tugged his head down, her soft smile tugging at his heart, before she kissed him.

Try as he might to keep things slow and steady, everything about her challenged that. Her scent, the kneading of her fingers on his back, the soft moans she made in her throat. And when she arched into him, Toben gave up. Need took over. His movements grew frenzied, each thrust deeper, harder, more driven. She clung to him, her moans hoarse and broken—pushing him to the edge.

His hand cupped her breast, stroking her nipple, his lips latching on until she fell apart. She cried out, long and hard. And her release sent him over the edge, his climax so hard he buried his face against her chest and moaned with its power.

Chapter Thirteen

Poppy was panting, her fingers still tangled in Toben's curls. He lay on top of her, his arms propping him over her, his head resting on her chest. She'd done what she swore she wouldn't do... And, right now, she'd do it again in a heartbeat. Her body hummed, still processing all sorts of amazing little twinges and aftershocks.

"You okay?" he asked. "I'm not sure I can move."

She laughed. "I'm good."

He lifted his head to look at her. "Glad to hear it." He stared at her, his hand smoothing her long hair from her cheek. "You're the most beautiful woman, Poppy White."

She smiled. "I guess I should feel flattered—considering how many women you've...known."

His smile faded, a little. "You're different."

She shook her head, determined to shut him down before her emotions could get just as out of control as her body. "You don't have to say pretty things to me, Toben. I don't expect—"

"Maybe I want to." He frowned. "I can't pretend my past didn't happen. I can say this, you and me, is different. And when I say you are the most beautiful thing I've ever seen, I mean it. Okay?"

His eyes searched hers, a hint of anxiety on his handsome face. He wanted her to believe him. But could she?

Her heart was banging, so damn happy she couldn't help but panic. "Okay," she whispered.

The corner of his mouth kicked up and he relaxed.

"What does *different* mean?" she asked, her hands sliding from his shoulders.

He shook his head and rolled off her, then plumped up the pillows and lay back, one arm tucked beneath his head.

"You brought it up." She rolled onto her stomach at his side, immediately distracted by his rock-hard body—on display and invitingly touchable. "You told Rowdy he could ask you anything."

He cocked a brow at her. "One, you're not Rowdy. Two, he'd never ask me about my screwed-up personal life."

"You're not happy? You seemed to enjoy the hell out of it. New bed, new gal, new…adventures." She couldn't imagine. Taking a man to bed was too intimate a thing to do so carelessly. Since Rowdy had been conceived, only Mitchell had shared her bed. And then it was to sleep, nothing more.

He lifted a long curl from her shoulder, twining it around his fingers as his gaze traveled over her bare shoulder. "So you're asking if I'm happy?"

She grinned. He really didn't want to talk about it. "Are you?"

"I don't think I could be happier than I am right now." His blue gaze met hers.

She swallowed.

"You don't trust me," he said, nodding. "I get it. But I'm not going anywhere. I want to be here, a family, for you both. I'm hoping I can prove I'm a different man. A better man than I was."

She rested her chin on her folded arms, watching him. He turned onto his side, his fingers running along her back and buttock, exploring her body with slow, gentle strokes. It was mesmerizing, easing her into a state of sensation.

His words repeated, over and over, until she accepted the truth. She wanted this; she wanted him to prove he was trustworthy. She wanted him. Not just for dinners and the occasional fireworks in her bedroom. But here, with her and Rowdy, every night—a real family bound by love and commitment. It was asking too much of him, she knew. She'd never seen evidence of commitment or love from the man, until now. If she were smart, she'd guard her heart and accept what she wanted could never happen. Still, she whispered, "What does that mean, Toben? A family?"

His hand stopped, resting on the base of her lower back. His breath powered from his chest, unsteady and harsh. "You, me and Rowdy."

She tried to sit up, but his arm snaked around her waist and tugged her against him.

"Don't start putting space between us now," he said.

She stared at his chest, willing her heart rate down.

"Poppy?" he whispered. "Look at me."

She shook her head.

"Please," he tried again.

It was a mistake. He was too damn mesmerizing, too intense. In his smile, she saw all the reasons she should run the other way. Passion, strength, charm—things that could hurt her in the end. Her hand rested on his chest, the racing of his heart pounding against her palm. That he couldn't fake. That was real. Even if she didn't know exactly what it meant.

"You know I love Rowdy?" he asked.

She nodded. Without a doubt.

"But you wouldn't believe me if I told you I love you." His fingers combed through her hair, his gaze traveling over her face. "Not yet. Not till I've shown you." His jaw tightened, pure resolve on his face. "And I will show you. Every day."

She swallowed. His words painted a pretty picture, one that made her ache. But...

"It's going to take time. Time, I've got." He smiled at her, tugging her close to press a kiss to her forehead. She relaxed, loving the way his hand smoothed down her back, the way he buried his nose in her hair to breathe her in. Like she was his—like he wanted her to be his.

"You staying?" she asked.

"Is that an invitation?" he asked.

"It's awful late to be driving home," she murmured, doing her best to avoid the question.

"Not really. I'll stay if you want me to."

She looked up at him. "Rowdy would want you to."

His grin was lethal. "That's a low blow, Miss White. Using our son like that." He tilted her head up. "Can't say it?"

She shot him a look.

He nodded. "Then I'll go." His grin faded. "I don't want to push this on you." He sat up and swung his legs over the side of the bed, leaving Poppy frantic.

She tugged her quilt up. She didn't want him to go. She wanted him to stay. Dammit, she needed him to stay. If he stayed, she couldn't talk herself into doubting him all over again. He stood, sliding his jeans up.

She grabbed the denim. "Stay, Toben."

He looked at her, the hurt on his face completely unexpected. She rose onto her knees, touching his cheek. His hand covered hers and he pressed a kiss to her palm.

"I want you to stay," she managed, even though her voice was wobbly and breathless.

He stared at her, his grin returning. "That hurt, didn't it?"

She sat back, blowing out a deep breath, and nodded.

He chuckled, dropping his jeans and climbing onto the

bed. His arms wrapped around her, tugging her against his side. "Come here, Poppy." He kissed her temple and held her close, the beat of his heart beneath her palm.

WEDNESDAY WAS A good day. He made pancakes on the griddle for Poppy and Rowdy, ate with them and left with a smile on his face. At six that evening, he got a text from his son, telling him there was fried chicken ready and waiting. He showered, packed a bag and headed to Poppy's.

Thursday morning, he rolled over to an empty bed and sat up, his heart in his throat. When she came in with a cup of coffee for him, he put it on the bedside table and pulled her to him. He kissed her with everything he had.

They had scrambled eggs and bacon, some toast and a lot of laughs before he made the drive to Boone Ranch. At five he offered to bring some pizzas out. They played cards and talked about painting Rowdy's room before bed. Then he loved Poppy long and hard into the early morning hours. She was sleeping when he headed out Friday morning. He left a plate of cinnamon rolls he'd picked up from Carl and Lola's on his way there the day before.

Driving to the ranch, he couldn't believe how lucky he was. Damn lucky. He was a smiling fool and he liked it.

"You're getting annoying." Deacon sighed when Toben walked into the ranch headquarters. "Good thing I'm hitting the road."

"If I was my usual self, you'd stay on longer?" Toben asked, knowing the truth.

Deacon grinned, shaking his head. "Nah, it's time."

Toben nodded. "Where are you headed?"

Deacon shrugged. "Might head to my dad's. Might not." He laughed.

Toben nodded. Deacon's dad was the exact opposite of Teddy Boone. Where Teddy was supportive and loving,

Woodrow Boone was loud, overbearing and best taken in small doses. He and Deacon had never seen eye to eye. After Deacon lost his family, Uncle Woodrow's answer had been for Deacon to move on and remarry quickly. But Deacon had loved his wife and kids and resented his father's callous dismissal of his grief.

Thinking about losing Rowdy and Poppy...Toben couldn't imagine it. It hurt too much to consider.

"Might head to New Mexico to Roger's place for a bit. Or out to California now that Chris has that new spread." Deacon shrugged. "Might just drive for a bit."

"When you leaving?"

"Tomorrow," Deacon answered. "Head out before the holiday crowds start pouring in. Figured I'd finish up some things around here so Archer can't complain."

"He's going to do that no matter what." Toben laughed.

"Speaking of Archer, he wants to see you," Deacon said.

Even a summons from his cousin wouldn't get to him today. "Okay. The family know you're going?"

Deacon shrugged. "Didn't want to make a big deal out of it."

Toben nodded and climbed into his truck. He drove the short distance between the ranch headquarters and the Boone Refuge administrative offices. Archer stood on the porch, talking to two of his wranglers. From the looks on the other men's faces, Archer was in a mood.

Toben sighed and climbed the steps of the building.

"Any questions?" Archer asked the two men.

They shook their heads, nodded at Toben and left.

"Morning," Toben said.

Archer nodded, watching the two men head to the barn. "New guys. I need you to show them the ropes."

Toben couldn't have been more surprised. "Okay."

Archer sighed, leveling him with a hard gaze. "The last

few weeks have been…good. You're working hard, setting a good pace and being an example for the others."

Toben could only stare at him.

"It's been pointed out that the refuge could benefit from having a foreman. I'm thinking you're it," Archer finished, his hands on his hips.

Toben continued to stare, speechless. Where the hell had this come from?

"You'll be on the road now and then, but you won't be away from your family too long. You know the job, this place, like the back of your hand." Archer nodded. "That's it."

Toben nodded. "All right. Thank you."

With another nod, Archer walked down the steps toward the barn.

Toben chuckled, rubbed his hand along the back of his neck and went to work.

Later, after Rowdy was tucked into bed and he and Poppy were sitting on the porch swing, he laughed. "I know he's short on people skills, but I'm pretty sure I've never been offered a job quite like that before."

Poppy smiled at him. "Congratulations."

He gave her feet a light squeeze, shifting them in his lap as he draped an arm along the back of the swing. "Thanks." He paused, hoping his next line of questioning wouldn't lead to friction. "Thought any more about getting a dog?"

Her brows rose. "Maybe."

"I'm not trying to kick a hornet's nest here," he said, stroking her ankles. "But Fisher, he's a veterinarian at the hospital, mentioned there were a few at the hospital needing homes."

"A few?" she asked.

"You don't have to take them all. Just see if one might fit." He chuckled. "When I'm on the road, it'd be nice to know y'all are protected."

Her eyes narrowed slightly. "Is that why you've been staying every night, Toben Boone? To protect us?"

He shook his head. "No, ma'am. I stay so I can take you to bed and make you moan." He cleared his throat, his words making him wish they were on the way to bed now. His thumb ran along the arch of her foot and she shivered. He smiled. "And I get to wake up my boy, see his smile first thing."

She shook her head.

"What?" he asked.

"You…you—" She stopped. "You're really happy?"

He nodded. "Yes, ma'am."

She studied him for some time before she whispered, "Me, too."

He tugged her into his lap then. "Good." He kissed her, soft and sweet.

They stay curled up until the night was black and only the fireflies and stars shed any light. The hoot of an owl, the distant snort of the horses and the whir of crickets put him at ease. She was happy. And he'd never been happier. Taking her to bed, he made sure every inch of her was screaming with happiness before he curled around her and slept.

The weekend was a blur. Poppy was getting ready for the grand opening and now that Archer had named him foreman, he was suddenly answering for a hell of a lot more than he'd expected. Sunday he fell asleep on the porch swing with Rowdy. And Monday Poppy had to shake him awake to get him to work on time.

He stumbled into the kitchen and poured himself a cup of coffee. Rowdy was making them toaster waffles while Poppy was on the porch, talking on the phone.

"Morning." Toben ruffled his hair, squeezing his shoulder. As far as Rowdy knew, Toben was staying in the guest room so he could spend more time with him. Something Rowdy wholeheartedly approved of. And, technically, it was true. Toben kept a bag there. But not much else. "Who's your mom talking to?" Toben asked, glancing at the clock. It was just after 6:00 a.m.

Rowdy shrugged. "Think it's Mitchell. You want syrup?"

"Yes, sir. I'll get it." He pulled the syrup from the pantry and set the table, trying not to worry about Poppy's phone call.

Poppy came in as they were sitting down. "Morning."

"Morning," he said, wishing he could kiss her. He knew, deep down, she and Mitchell were just friends. But that didn't stop him from being jealous.

She smiled at him. "I was telling Rowdy about the dogs at the hospital."

Toben nodded, smiling. "Wanna go look?" he asked. "How about we head over there after I get off work? We can go after your ma's grand opening."

"Not too late?" Rowdy asked, his excitement barely contained.

Toben shook his head. "No, sir, I know people."

"Sound good?" Poppy asked.

Rowdy nodded, smiling from ear to ear.

"What time do things get started tonight?" Toben asked.

"At six," Poppy said. "Don't feel like you have to be there."

He glanced at her. "I don't."

"He wants to be there, Ma," Rowdy offered.

"Yep," Toben agreed, arching a brow at Poppy. His boy knew him well.

Poppy's cheeks grew pink, her smile so sweet it took everything he had not to pull her up for a kiss. "Okay."

He finished his waffles, washed his plate and grabbed his hat. "I'll see you two tonight."

"Bye, Dad. Have a good day." Rowdy waved.

He caught sight of Poppy and winked. "It already is, Rowdy."

Chapter Fourteen

Poppy tried to remember who was who. Cutter, the outspoken old man who owned the bar, was unforgettable. So were Carl and Lola. Though she could tell Lola was a gossip—well-meaning but a gossip all the same. She met the Johanssons from the diner, the bank manager, several of the volunteer firefighters, a few teachers, the town's only lawyer and several Boones.

Annabeth Boone was the elementary school principal. A gorgeous woman married to an equally handsome man, Ryder Boone. Ryder owned the only garage in town. Not only did they welcome her with open arms, but their oldest boy, Cody, and Rowdy were instant friends.

"Can I take Cody up to the office?" Rowdy asked.

Poppy nodded. "Sure. Might be quieter up there."

"And less grown-ups," Rowdy added.

The upstairs apartment was still a work in progress. She had a desk set up, a sofa and television. The bathroom worked but the two bedrooms were used for storage. Rowdy kept a box of toys, books and blocks there for those days he was forced to stay late with her. Not that he ever complained.

"How are you settling in?" Annabeth asked. "Not too quiet a life?"

Poppy shook her head. "I like it, honestly. I know it's better for Rowdy, too."

"Added bonus is having his dad close," Ryder jumped in. "Where is he?"

"Archer's probably kept him late." Renata arrived, leaning in to hug them each. "Looks like a great turnout, Poppy."

"I can't get over this place," Annabeth agreed. "Last time I was in here I was afraid I'd go through the floor."

Poppy nodded. "There was some wood rot, plumbing issues, some wiring issues…but I think it's turned out… perfect." She was proud of the place and the work she'd done to make it just right. "Now it's time to fix up the homestead."

Ryder nodded. "The Travis place was creaky a few years back. But the land…"

She nodded. "I've never seen more beautiful country," she agreed. "I can work with the house."

"I can help," Ryder offered. "Since we're family and all."

Annabeth nodded. "You should have seen our place, Poppy. But Ryder—" the look of pure adoration she sent her husband made Poppy smile, though she was more than a little envious "—made my dreams come true."

"Course I did." Ryder took her hand.

Poppy laughed with the other women, her attention wandering around the room. Everyone seemed to be having a good time. It warmed her through that these people had come out to welcome her and recognized the time and effort she'd put into turning the shop into something special.

The door opened, catching her eye. Toben walked in, all starched and pressed and so handsome her lungs emptied. His blue gaze found hers, his answering smile downright dangerous.

"About time," Ryder said.

Toben nodded. "Had to get cleaned up. And pick up Tandy."

Poppy stared at the woman who'd come in with him. The woman stared right back. She looked a lot like Toben, bright blue eyes and a winning smile. But Tandy seemed calm, a word she'd never use to describe Toben.

"Archer working you like a dog?" Ryder laughed.

"No picking on Archer, you two." Renata sighed. "How's it going? Mr. Foreman?"

She was acutely aware of Toben coming to her side, standing close before he answered. "Pretty damn good." He smiled at her. "Looks like a nice turnout."

She nodded, fully aware all eyes were on them.

"Poppy, this is my sister, Tandy." He nodded at his twin. "Tandy, this is Poppy."

Tandy enveloped her in a hug. And for some reason, Poppy wanted to cry.

"I'm glad to meet you, Poppy." Tandy kept on hugging her. "So glad."

"You, too," she managed, hugging the woman back.

"Where's Rowdy?" Toben asked.

Tandy stepped back, her expression mirroring one she'd seen on her boy's face so many times. She was excited— and nervous.

"He's upstairs with Cody," Poppy said.

"I'll take her?" Toben asked.

Poppy nodded, not wanting to overwhelm Rowdy. She blinked, willing the sting of tears away. She wasn't one for tears. Especially when she was in a room full of professionals. And people who had claimed her as family—even though she wasn't. Maybe that was it. This sort of love and support didn't exist in her world.

She'd invited Rose and Bob out of obligation, knowing they wouldn't come. They were, as expected, busy. Mitchell had called to say he wasn't sure when he'd get there but he'd try not to miss the fanfare later this week. She had mixed emotions about that. Now that things had changed between her and Toben, she knew things would likely change with her and Mitchell, too.

Toben came back shortly, his hand a soothing presence on the base of her spine. "She's on the floor with them. Blocks are everywhere."

Poppy smiled. It was nice to hear Rowdy had an aunt willing to get on the floor to play. Her eyes were stinging again.

"If you two ever need a babysitter, Tandy is the best," Annabeth offered. "She's handled all three of our boys on her own a few times."

You two? The words made Poppy uneasy.

"And lived," Ryder joined in.

"They're much easier when you tag-team them," Renata volunteered. "Rowdy'd be a piece of cake. No offense."

"None taken." Ryder laughed.

If you two ever need a babysitter. She excused herself, forcing herself to mingle with the rest of her guests. Honestly, she was panicking. It was one thing to play house, alone and away from the rest of the world. But here, with so many of Stonewall Crossing's residents out in force, she wasn't sure she wanted to be so intimately tied to Toben. If he left, it would be that much harder.

There was a very large part of her that was beginning to believe he might, possibly, care for her—not just their son. But the rest of her, the part she'd been listening to for seven years, refused to believe it.

She listened as the bank manager rattled off loan options to fix up the Travis homestead. Not that she needed a loan. Her career had ensured she and Rowdy would be taken care of through whatever life might throw at them.

And now, with the shop, she hoped she'd bring in something monthly she could invest—for Rowdy's future.

As the evening went on, Poppy did her best to keep smiling, talking and working the room. People were looking forward to tomorrow—seeing Poppy White lead in the Grand Entry was a big deal. She'd almost backed out, but Rowdy had pulled her rodeo trunk from the back of her closet and she'd given up. His enthusiasm was hard to refuse. And, as he pointed out, if there was anyone who didn't know about her and her shop, the emcee would be sure to tell everyone who came out for the rodeo. So it was good for business.

The shop had nearly emptied out by eight, so Poppy started cleaning up. Cutter, who was full of opinions, shook her hand and said, "You'll do well here, Miss Poppy. Got yourself a real pretty little place." He grinned. "And your boy is a Boone—good family. Looks like you and Toben are picking up right where you left off." He touched the brim of his hat and left her, her pulse racing and skin clammy.

Right where you left off... The man had no idea what he'd said. He had no way of knowing what sort of horrible, lonely memories his words would stir. But now that he'd said it, that was all she could think about. Waking up disappointed to find him gone. She'd been foolish to think he'd stay but she'd hoped nonetheless. It'd hurt, but finding out she was pregnant had been worse. And trying to find Toben, being so scared she didn't know which way was up, had brought her to her knees. Add to it Rose's assurance that Poppy couldn't raise a child with her lifestyle, that she and Bob would take the baby... Their relationship had never been the same. Hell, her life had never been the same.

The Boones lingered, helping her tidy up until the shop was clean and she was ready to close up. All she wanted was quiet, time to calm down. Alone.

"I'll go get Rowdy," Toben offered.

"I'll go," she said, brushing past him. She didn't want more time with the Boones. She wanted her son—to herself.

She climbed the stairs and paused in the doorway of the sitting room. Tandy Boone lay on her back on the floor holding up a book. Cody had left with his parents, but Rowdy lay beside her, listening while she read a story about a pony named Fritz and how heroic he was. It was one of his favorite stories. Rowdy said Fritz was just like Cheeto, loyal and fearless.

"You okay?" She jumped—she hadn't heard Toben follow her up the stairs.

She nodded.

He pulled her into his arms, tugging her into the shadows of the hall. "I'm proud of you." He brushed her lips with his. "You did this, Poppy. All of this."

She looked up at him, unable to make sense of the jumble of emotions tangled up inside. Being in his arms helped. And that made it ten times worse. "I'm scared," she confessed.

He froze. "Of what?"

She blew out a long breath... *Everything.* "Where do I start?"

He tilted her head back, stroking her cheek. "Wherever you want."

She shook her head, regret flooding her. She shouldn't have said anything. Not now. When she was vulnerable. She pushed against him until he let her go. "I guess it's just...a big night and all."

"Poppy—"

"We should get Rowdy if we're going to look at dogs," she interrupted. She'd figure this out on her own. At the end of the day, the only person she could count on was herself. Life had taught her that.

TOBEN KNEW SOMETHING had happened, but he wasn't sure what it was. One minute she'd been smiling; the next she'd seemed withdrawn and defensive. He'd hoped her fear was gone after the week they'd shared. But she was determined to keep him out of her heart.

Rowdy, in all his childlike wonder, was oblivious to the tension on the ride to the veterinary hospital. "I figure a real small dog doesn't make much sense for protection," he was saying.

"Ya never know," Toben argued. "They call them ankle biters for a reason."

Rowdy giggled.

"Let's wait and see what there is." Poppy laughed, too— no way to resist their son's giggle.

"It's a big decision, Rowdy." Toben nodded. "You need to trust this dog. You need to know he or she is going to take care of you."

"How will I know?" Rowdy asked.

"Instinct," Toben said. "Most of these dogs were dropped off by previous owners. Some were animals that were injured and left. Lots of college kids around here adopt animals, then turn them loose or dump them when they realize they don't have the time or money to take care of them."

"Poor things." Poppy's voice was wistful.

Toben nodded. Animals were family to Rowdy and Poppy—he knew that. To leave one behind was unthinkable. "So make sure they're the right one before you pick. Some of these guys have all but given up on finding a forever home."

Rowdy grew serious for the last bit of the ride.

The three of them arrived at the hospital when it was dark. He entered through the front doors, nodding at the three students at the desk.

"They're still open?" Poppy asked as they walked through the staff-only entrance. "Can we go back here?"

"Yep. They're fourth-year students. They have to take emergency-duty shifts, just like med students."

"Take a lot of schooling to be a veterinarian?" Rowdy asked.

Toben nodded. "But that's good. It's a big job, so you have to know a lot."

Rowdy nodded.

"My cousins Hunter, Fisher and Archer are all veterinarians. And your aunt Tandy is studying real hard to be one, too." He winked at Rowdy. "That's why they know me around here."

Rowdy nodded. "You ever want to be one?"

Toben shook his head. "Can't imagine not spending most hours outside. Or in the saddle. It makes me sad to think about it." Which was true.

He led them into the break room. Fisher was on emergency duty tonight and had been the one to tell them to come on over, no matter how late.

"Well, Rowdy, it's plain to see who your daddy is." He held out his hand to the boy. "I'm your cousin Fisher. Nice to meet you."

"You, too, sir," Rowdy said, shaking his hand. "I got a little of Ma in me, too."

"That you do, Rowdy." He smiled at Poppy, offering his hand. "Fisher Boone."

"Poppy," she said, shaking his hand—that same sad look in her eyes. "Thank you for having us here, now…"

Fisher nodded. "Dogs don't keep business hours." He grinned. "Or cats or lizards or any animal, for that matter." He led them down the hall, leading them through several rooms with cages, medical equipment and anything a veterinarian could possibly need. "I've got a few real friendly ones you might want to meet."

But Rowdy paused by the first cage. "Who's that?"

Fisher backed up. "She's a sweet thing. But she's a little skittish."

Rowdy dropped to his knees. "Hey, girl," he said. "Hi."

Toben watched his son, his small hand extended toward the black dog huddled in the corner. "She okay?" he asked, hoping Fisher understood what he was asking. No way he was going to let his son near an unpredictable animal.

Fisher nodded. "She's shy. A real shadow, follows real close, real quiet."

"Maybe not the best guard dog," he said softly to his son.

"Sure she is," Rowdy said. "Come on, I'm real nice. So is Ma."

The dog's ears perked up, her head tilting one way, then the next.

"Come on," Rowdy said.

Poppy knelt beside her son. "She's a pretty girl."

The dog ran toward the gate then and flopped on her back, baring her tummy. Toben chuckled. "Well, that's some greeting. Can I open the gate?"

"Go for it," Fisher said.

The dog sat up, watching him. As soon as the gate was open, she rushed to Rowdy and climbed into his lap. Rowdy giggled, knocked back onto his rear. "You're too big, girl," he said, stroking along the dog's neck.

Toben thought the dog was just the right size for Rowdy. She had some Border collie in her, with thick glossy black fur, wise brown eyes and alert pointed ears. Her tail wooshed, her long fur fanning Rowdy's hair back. Toben chuckled and looked at Poppy and his heart stopped. She had tears in her eyes, her smile so wide and bright he knew he'd love her until his heart stopped beating.

"I guess she's it," Poppy said.

"Feel free to look around," Fisher said.

"She might need a friend, Ma," Rowdy piped up.

Poppy sighed, shaking her head. "She'll have us, Rowdy. I think she'll be happy with that."

"And Cheeto," Toben added. "Something tells me she and Cheeto will get along great." If for no other reason than they both loved his boy so much. The black dog gave Poppy a sniff, licked her hand and hurried back to Rowdy. "She's good."

"Can she come home tonight, Ma?" Rowdy asked.

Toben saw her look his way. He nodded once, saw her lips tighten and frowned. What the hell had he done? And how could he undo it?

"We don't have anything at the house," she answered. "And we won't be home tomorrow night, Rowdy. Seems wrong to take her home now and leave her alone for most of the day tomorrow. If we knew how she was with crowds, we could take her. But I don't want to upset her."

Rowdy nodded. "You're right, Ma. Can we come get her after that? Please?"

"Would that be okay?" Poppy asked Fisher. "I hate to leave her so long but—"

"No, sounds like the best thing," Fisher agreed. "I'll let Hunter know you two will be coming in. He's the one on call."

"Thank you," Poppy answered.

Saying goodbye to the dog wasn't easy, but Toben offered to bring him back to visit tomorrow so the dog wouldn't worry too much.

"You can drop us at the shop," Poppy said. "My truck is there. No reason for you to have to make the trip. Besides, I'm sure you're ready for a night back in your own bed."

Toben shot her a look, but she kept her eyes straight

ahead. He couldn't very well argue with her, not with Rowdy in the truck. And she knew it. But if she thought he was going to the bunkhouse, tail tucked between his legs, she was in for a surprise.

Chapter Fifteen

Poppy spread Rowdy's blankets around him, pressing a kiss to his cheek and smoothing the curls back from his forehead. He was well on his way to dreamland, but she stayed by his side. Tonight had been good—and horrible. She'd met nice people, people who wanted to include her in their lives. They'd found a sweet dog that Poppy knew would watch over her son and keep them safe. Rowdy had met more of his family, a family eager to welcome him into their hearts.

And she'd been reminded of all the damage and heart-break Toben was capable of. How had she let this happen? How had she let her defenses down—put her and Rowdy in jeopardy? She knew better.

Rowdy snorted in his sleep and rolled onto his side. She smiled, stood and left. She glanced down the hall at the empty house. Being lonely was a way of life for her. After Toben, she'd learned guarding her heart was the best course of action. One she couldn't afford to change now. It wasn't *if* she and Toben didn't work out; it was when. Rowdy deserved better.

She went to her room, cursing to herself as she stripped down, then took a long, hot shower. When the water ran cold, she dried off and tugged on one of the shirts Toben had left. She hugged herself, burying her nose in the sleeve as she walked from the bathroom to her bedroom. *No. Seeking comfort in Toben Boone makes me a fool.* Frustration gripped her by the throat as she yanked the shirt up and off and tossed it into the corner and slid into a robe. She knew him, knew how he operated. Yes, he said and did the right things. He always had. Always.

She grabbed a pillow off the bed, punched it once and kicked it into the corner.

"What'd the pillow ever do to you?" Toben leaned in the doorframe, fully dressed and scowling.

Poppy jumped…swallowing down her startled cry. "What the hell…" She pressed a hand to her chest, her heart thumping like mad.

He pushed off the doorframe and crossed the room until he was standing so close—but not touching her. And dammit, she wanted his arms around her. Even now, knowing she was a fool. Instead his hands stayed firmly planted on his hips, his face lined with irritation. Like he had a right to be irritated.

His words were low. "What the hell was that all about, Poppy? What happened?"

She swallowed. "I…need space."

His posture eased but he still didn't reach for her. "Why?"

Was he nervous? "Why? Because we're not used to all this. I…I'm not used to sharing him, Toben. It's just been us for so long." She glanced at him, too nervous to hold his gaze. She didn't want to lose her anger, to get sucked into those baby blues or the hope they stirred in her. "Now all these people have a claim on him. And I'm just—"

His hands clasped her arms. "You're everything to him."

She shrugged out of his hold, his touch too tempting.

He frowned, a deep furrow forming between his brows. "There's no reason to feel threatened, Poppy. There's room for them in this family, too."

"*They* don't threaten me," she whispered, then cleared her throat. She met his gaze, watching as his expression hardened.

"I do?" he asked, crossing his arms. "All I want is—"

"I know what you want," she cut him off. "What you say you want. And maybe, right now, you do want it—us, I mean. But dammit, Toben…" She shook her head. "You left me. You were unreachable, gone, disappeared, a ghost, when I *needed* you. You knew me. You let me think I was special…" She broke off. Baring her soul wasn't something she did. All the words she'd ever wanted to say to him seemed to get tangled and twisted and incoherent. "Why is now any different? With me? I understand you want Rowdy in your life. But me?" She shook her head. "I'm the same person you left sleeping in that hotel room years ago. The same woman. I might have let my loneliness blindside me a little but… You didn't want me then. I'd be a fool to think you want me now. And I'm not a fool."

He shook his head. "Poppy, you think this is all about getting you into bed?" His voice had turned gruff.

"No." She hugged herself tight. "I think it was about you needing to feel close to Rowdy—maybe even to me since I know him best. But that's all. And pretending there's something else going on is dangerous."

His jaw flexed. "Because?"

She swallowed. "You're you and I'm me."

His eyes narrowed. "Meaning what?"

"You leave. I can't. You leave me, you leave Rowdy. Whatever happens, I won't let Rowdy get—"

"Hurt," he finished. His face was hard. "So this, us, doesn't matter?"

"There's no us, Toben. This was…sex. You've slept with enough women to know that. We have a son, period."

He touched her cheek, smoothing her damp hair from her shoulder. "You think that's all there is between us?"

She nodded, refusing to step back, to flinch away from him.

There was sadness on his face, in his beautiful blue eyes. "You said you were scared earlier. I never thought you were scared of me."

He had no right to look at her like that, no right to make her heart hurt.

"You're trying to shut me out."

"No, I'm trying to move on." She stepped around him. "We had unfinished business. Now we don't."

"There's no moving on from this, Poppy. Not for me, anyway." His tone was soft and oh so tempting. "You won't believe me, but I know everything I want is here."

She was unable to face him now. She wasn't that strong. "This doesn't need to be difficult, Toben. No one's going to be heartbroken here. Except, maybe, our son."

Silence stretched on until Poppy's heart was in her throat. Why wouldn't he just leave? Why couldn't he accept the truth, for everyone's sake?

"You're wrong." The floor squeaked as he came around her, staring down at her. "I messed up. Big-time. I had you and I didn't understand how important you were—not yet. After three years, I thought our night together would be another good time. I woke up and life was upside down. I hightailed it out of there, too scared to think things through. I was always looking for you—to see you, to avoid you…"

Her heart thumped. He'd looked for her?

"After that, I stayed drunk for a good six months. Deacon snapped me out of it, sobered me up and told me to get over you, find someone else. I looked, believe me. But none of them were you." He paused. "I'm an idiot for ripping up your letters and a chickenshit for never returning your calls. I didn't understand then what you mean to me. Now I know. And now that I've found you, I'm not letting go without a fight."

For an instant, his words filled all the cracks and holes her heart bore. Too bad she knew they were a desperate attempt to hold on to her until he was ready to cut her loose. She couldn't go through that again, not with Rowdy relying on her. "Stop, Toben. I...I need you to leave."

"I love you, Poppy." The words were rough. "Whether you believe me or not, I want you to know it."

Poppy pressed her eyes shut, digging deep for the strength to send him away.

"You hear me?" he asked.

She looked up at him, her words thick. "I hear you."

"Want me to go?"

She almost shook her head. If only she could believe him...love him. But loving him was a risk, the biggest risk of her life. Would he still love her once he knew she loved him? Or was it the challenge that kept him around? Confessing how she felt opened the door to a pain she wasn't sure she could bear. For her and Rowdy.

She wanted to believe him. Nothing would make her happier than knowing his love was real. But her fear and anger had been so well tended the last few years she didn't know how to trust in him. No matter how much she wanted to.

"Yes. I want you to go."

She hadn't expected the anguish on his face. Or the slicing pain in her heart as he left her feeling more alone than she'd ever been before.

"CHEETO LOOKS GOOD." Toben smiled, adjusting the pony's girth and double-checking Rowdy's stirrups. "Before long, we'll need to get you on a horse. One that will be a friend for you and Cheeto."

Rowdy grinned. "Think so?"

Toben nodded. "When you come to the ranch, you can see what I do. We have a lot of horses needing homes. Like your dog. What are you going to call her?"

"I like Lady or Cheyenne. Ma likes Cheyenne." Rowdy said. "She said it was a special place."

Toben patted his son's leg. "It is." Cheyenne, Wyoming, was where Rowdy was made. Cheyenne was where he'd fallen in love with and then lost Poppy. "It's a good name."

Rowdy nodded.

"Don't you two look like peas in a pod?" Renata sat on her roan, her saddle and bridle decorated with red, white and blue ribbons—like everyone else's. "Handsome as all get-out."

Toben nodded. He'd searched high and low until he'd found matching shirts for him and Rowdy. In Poppy's shop, of course. "We look good."

"Think he gets his looks from his mom," Renata said, winking.

He nodded. Poppy was a beauty. All day he'd struggled with the deep hurt of her rejection, but he understood. If she couldn't trust him, it was his fault. She'd seen how he lived, up close and personal, and knew he was a rat bastard. Had been. Not anymore. He had two options: give up a future with her or show her he'd changed. Put that way, there was only one choice.

Rowdy giggled, tipping his hat at Renata. "Thank you, ma'am."

Renata exchanged a look with Toben, smiling broadly. "That, right there, is how a real cowboy talks to a lady."

Toben beamed with pride, swinging up into his saddle beside his son. He was riding one of the refuge horses. The white horse had been painted with chalk, a faux firework across his haunch and back legs. Renata's handiwork. "You ready to show them how it's done?" he asked.

Rowdy nodded. "Yes, sir. Where's Ma?" he asked, turning in his saddle.

"I know your ma. She won't be late." Toben guided the horse in line. For Poppy White, rodeo was serious business.

Rowdy nodded. "She's nervous about tonight. Holding the flag and all."

Toben thought about the scars on her side. He hoped she wouldn't argue with him about the alteration he'd made on the saddle. He didn't want her to hurt if she didn't have to. And this should help, if she'd use it.

Poppy arrived moments later, sitting pretty on Stormy, her red sequined top sparkling in the Texas sun. She wore a white hat, secured beneath her chin with a bright blue cord. Her jeans hugged her in all the right places, making Toben curse and shift in his saddle.

"Boys," she said, smiling at Rowdy—barely glancing his way.

"Hold up," Renata said. "Smile." She took several pictures. "Y'all look great."

Toben stared at Poppy, his heart so full.

Her brown eyes met his, widening. "What?"

"Nothing," he said. Telling her he was a damn lucky man would get her all riled up. He didn't want that, not today.

"Smile and wave," she said, winking at Rowdy before nudging Stormy forward.

He and Rowdy followed. Cheeto was having to trot to keep up with the larger horses, so Toben slowed his horse to a leisurely walk. Cheeto could breathe easier.

"Dad." Rowdy looked at him. "I was wondering if you were going to marry Ma?"

Toben looked at his son. He hoped, in time, Poppy might trust him enough—love him enough—to consider the notion. "Someday, I hope. There's nothing I want more. Is that all right with you? Since you're the man of the house and all."

Rowdy looked at him, long and hard. "You'll treat her right? Won't hurt her or run out on us?"

Toben looked his son in the eye. "Only way I'd go is if she asked me to—"

"Even then. You ask her, it has to be forever." Rowdy shook his head. "Uncle Bob said marriage is hard work."

"He's right," he agreed. He imagined marriage to Rose might be harder than marriage to Poppy. But it was true. He wanted Poppy to have his name, to be his. But no matter what happened between them, he'd be there for them.

"Ma didn't marry Mitchell, because she'll never break a promise, not ever." He paused. "But I think she loves you that way. Like you love her."

"I hope so, Rowdy." His son's words eased the ache in his heart.

"I can help find a ring," Rowdy offered. "You should propose with a nice ring."

Toben nodded. He didn't want to ding his boy's enthusiasm, but he knew what Poppy's answer would be right now. "Let's keep it a surprise."

Rowdy nodded.

The parade went off without a hitch. He and Rowdy waved and threw candy and red, white and blue beaded necklaces until their arms ached.

When they made their way to the Stonewall Crossing fairgrounds, they were swapping jokes and laughing. Until he saw Mitchell Lee with Poppy in his arms.

"Hey, look, it's Mitchell." Rowdy waved.

Toben nodded, forcing a smile on his face. "Your ma was worried he wouldn't make it." He rode up to the fence, making a decision to be the man's best friend if he had to.

He was indebted to Mitchell, if nothing else. The man had taken care of his son and the woman he loved when no one else had—himself included.

He swung down from the saddle, secured both his horse and Cheeto to the fence and swung Rowdy down. Rowdy grabbed his hand and tugged him after him.

Mitchell hugged Rowdy. "How's it going? I caught a glimpse of you bringing up the rear with Cheeto. Looked good, mighty good."

"Mitchell." Toben held out his hand.

Mitchell shot a quick glance at Poppy before shaking his hand. "Boone."

Toben let it go, figuring the best thing to do in this situation was give them space. "I'll take the horses back. Get Cheeto settled for you." He touched his hat, smiling at Poppy.

"You don't have to," Poppy said.

"I know. I'll see you later on." He untied Cheeto and led the pony to his truck and horse trailer. "I know *you* like me better," he said to Cheeto, leading the pony inside.

He drove out to Poppy's first, where he put the pony in his stall, fed him and gave him a solid rubdown before heading to Boone Ranch. He was unloading horses when Renata arrived with the other truck and trailer.

A few ranch hands helped unload, storing saddles, brushing out coats and turning the horses out to graze. He and Renata worked together until she finally asked, "What's the guy to her?"

"Her friend," he answered.

"You like him?"

He shrugged. "I don't really know him. But he's been a good friend to Poppy, so I guess so."

"So you don't like him, but you're playing nice? Guess

that means things are getting serious between you two?" she asked.

"I'm sure as hell trying." He looked at her, confessing, "I'm in way over my head."

Renata grinned. "You? Mr. One-Night-Wonderland?"

Toben winced. "That's part of the problem." He had been with a lot of women, some he didn't remember. The nickname was offensive, but it was true. One night, period. Except for Poppy. She'd never faded from his mind. And now, every time he was with her, he knew he was where he was meant to be. Her scent eased him. Her voice called to him. He responded to her—instinctively, primally and completely. He nodded.

"Hate to say it, but I can understand her hesitancy." Renata patted his shoulder, sighing. "While you're trying to figure out how to win her over, help me out, too. Are there any decent men left in town for me to date? It's not fair. I have to leave Stonewall Crossing to get a date. Too many brothers for a fellow in these parts to man up."

Toben frowned at her. "It's not just brothers, Renata." He loved Renata like she were his sister. But, like his sister, he didn't know a man worthy of her time and affection. Frankly, he was prepared to kick ass and take names if any of the men he knew tried. At the same time, he didn't want Renata or Tandy lonely and unloved.

Renata laughed. "A gal gets lonely, Toben."

"I know." His frown grew. "I've met plenty of them."

"Don't worry." Renata sighed. "I'm not adventurous enough to be one of those women. Poppy's friend is a good-looking man, but I don't think I need to tell you that." She looked at him. "And since he's only a *friend*, I might just have to introduce myself to him."

Toben looked at his cousin. He might not want Mitchell

Lee hanging around Poppy, but Renata… That could work. "You won't have to. I'll introduce you to him."

Renata grinned. "Even though I know there's an ulterior motive, I'm going to smile and say thank you."

Toben chuckled. "You're welcome."

Chapter Sixteen

Poppy stared again at the tooled leather bracket now affixed to her saddle. It was rigid, the opening perfect for the slim aluminum pole. She wouldn't have to hold it as tight or brace it against her side. It would cut back on drag, easing most of the resistance of the flag. Meaning her side wouldn't be on fire. He'd done this for her—to take care of her.

"Isn't that fancy?" Mitchell said, following her gaze and inspecting the bracket. "He's trying hard, isn't he?"

Poppy nodded.

"And succeeding?" he asked, his smile genuine.

She frowned. "Give me some credit, Mitchell."

"Can you trust him? That's what counts, Poppy." He sighed. "I'm not going to be around as much now—"

"Mitchell," she interrupted him. "I love you. I'm always going to. You're my best friend."

Mitchell smiled at her. "A fact I don't take for granted."

She nodded. "But…I want you to be his friend, too. Rowdy shouldn't have to choose."

"Okay." He sighed, heavily. "I give you my word I'll try."

"Not to keep tabs. But a real friend." She put her hands on her hips. "I'm sort of hoping he'll stay around. For Rowdy—not me."

"Not you?" He sighed, eyeing the bracket on her saddle. "I'll *try*."

"Lend a girl a hand? And go get into your fancy box." She let him help her into the saddle and smiled at him. "And congratulations on the new job, Mr. Fancy-Emcee-*and*-Rodeo-Production-Manager. You're a big important person now."

He arched an eyebrow. "I thought I always was."

She laughed. "Go on." She turned Stormy and let the horse circle the pasture a few times. Her gaze wandered to the horizon, the pinks and blues turning a deep purple as the sun disappeared from sight.

She sucked in a deep breath, a mix of nerves and adrenaline running through her veins. She wasn't competing tonight, but it didn't matter. The lights, the sounds, the smells—rodeo woke her up, and nothing else mattered.

She turned Stormy, her gaze sweeping the stands. Rowdy was there somewhere, sitting with Tandy and Cody. She'd given him money for a funnel cake and lemonade and knew he's be a sticky mess by the time she made it back to the stands. But that was okay—bedtime was hours away. Once the rodeo was over and the dance was done, they'd watch the fireworks.

"Good evening, ladies and gentlemen, and welcome to Stonewall Crossing's Fourth of July Rodeo Festival. My name is Doug Davison and I'm joined tonight by one of PRCA's finest emcees, Mitchell Lee." The speaker crackled.

"Nice to be here." Mitchell's voice rolled over her, making her smile. "I've never seen a sunset so patriotic before. Will you look at that? Red, white and blue. Makes my heart beat a little stronger."

She spun Stormy in a circle, kicking up her pace. Not much longer before the big entrance. After two more loops, she urged Stormy to the gate.

Four young women waited on horseback, each carrying an American flag.

"Here you are, Miss White." One of the wranglers held up the larger flag, helping her slide it through the bracket on her saddle and into the base on her stirrup.

"Miss White," one of the girls said. "It's a real honor to ride with you."

The other three joined in, reminding her how magical it had been when she'd met the women she'd looked up to. Suzanne Carlson, Judy Hailey and Brenna Woods. She'd stared at them, hoping her career would be half as impressive as theirs had been. She was humbled to hear these young ladies talk, to answer their questions and promise that—once they were done—she'd be happy to sit down and talk to them some more.

They did two loops to warm up and burst through the gate into the arena.

She and Stormy led, flying around the fence, then cutting into a figure-eight pattern. It was exhilarating, the speed of her horse and the wind in her hair. She heard the whistles, knew Mitchell was building up the crowd's enthusiasm. And Rowdy and Toben were watching them. She wanted to make them proud. The four other riders kept circling, but Poppy swung around and trotted back into the center of the arena.

"Ladies and gentlemen, as we stare upon the flag of our great nation, let us stand and sing the national anthem." Mitchell's voice was solemn. "Here to lead us is Stonewall Crossing's own Miss Nina Garza."

When the last chorus began, Poppy had Stormy kneel. It was what they'd always done, and it seemed right. The crowd went wild.

One more turn around the arena and she and Stormy trotted out.

She handed off the flag and trotted the field twice, the girls trotting right along with her. Once the horses were cooled down, she headed for her truck and trailer. Toben was waiting. She could do this. The two of them were always going to be part of one another's lives; they had a son to raise together. Her gaze fell to the bracket he'd attached to her saddle. His thoughtfulness had touched her. *Dammit.*

"Need a hand?" he asked.

She hesitated. Being close to him was bad. But her side was sore and she could use the help. "Yes, please." She swung from the saddle. He caught her, his hands on her waist, easing her down against his chest until she was on her feet.

"You looked mighty pretty out there, Poppy. You and Stormy are a perfect team." His voice was low, his hands light on her waist.

It would be all too easy to slide her arms around his neck. Instead she stepped back, out of his hold. His disappointment was visible. She resisted the urge to touch him, stammering, "I-It might not have gone so well if not for you."

His nod was stiff. "Rowdy said your side pulled sometimes. Didn't want you hurting."

She shoved her hands in her pockets, fighting the urge to reach up and push off his hat, to kiss him until they were breathing hard and rattled. "Thank you," she managed.

"Poppy, I—"

"We should find Rowdy," she interrupted. Her emotions were wound too tight, too raw, to stay here—alone—with Toben. Even though she'd made her decision, her heart wasn't on the same page.

"Lead the way," he said. "He have a favorite event?"

She shook her head. "It changes. Sometimes it's bulls, sometimes it's broncs." She paused. "He's with Tandy and

Cody. He and Cody sure have hit it off," she said, trying to keep their conversation easy.

"Cody's a good boy, and so is Rowdy. They get it from their mothers," he said, smiling at her as they walked to the arena. "You're a good mother, Poppy. And a good woman. The sort of woman that deserves the love of a good man. Still, can't stop hoping you'll settle for me and give our family a chance."

His words made her heart long for that very thing.

TOBEN DIDN'T SEE much of the rodeo. Between Poppy and Rowdy, he was preoccupied. His son was heading into the ring for Mutton Bustin' when they found Tandy.

"They both wanted to go," she explained, pointing out Cody and Rowdy entering the arena.

"He takes this pretty seriously," Poppy said. "He was asking about the calf scramble earlier this week. Luckily, he's too young."

Toben nodded. He didn't want to think about Rowdy being stomped on by teenage boys and steers. He was mighty, but he was little.

Cody fell off the sheep quick, winding up with a mouthful of dirt. He popped up, smiling and unhurt. They clapped, relieved.

"Watch," Poppy said, pointing at their son.

Rowdy had a fearsome grip, his hands holding tight to the wool around the sheep's neck. Rowdy made it all the way to the end of the arena. But he didn't let go. The sheep spun around and headed right back to the beginning, and Rowdy stuck like glue.

Toben laughed. "That's a man determined."

"Can't imagine where he gets it," Tandy said.

Toben looked at Poppy. "Much as I'd like to take the

credit, I think Rowdy might have a double dose. His ma is pretty tough, too."

Poppy smiled, taking it as the compliment he'd intended.

Rowdy won, no doubt about it. Three men had to chase the sheep down, and Rowdy held on the whole time. When he arrived back at the stand, he smelled like dirt and sheep and was on an adrenaline high.

Amid the congratulations and pats on the back, Rowdy recounted every second of his ride. Toben listened, loving every expression on his son's face. To see him so animated, so proud, was something he knew he'd treasure for years to come.

His attention wandered to Poppy, sparkling beneath the lights—smiling so sweetly at their son that his heart hurt. What would it be like to take her hand? For her to be his and everyone here to know it… He wanted that. He wanted his son to have a whole family, a father who loved his mother, who loved their family and never let them down.

"Don't you think?" Rowdy asked him.

"I didn't hear that last part," he said, leaning forward.

"I said Cody didn't get a good sheep," Rowdy repeated, loudly, in his ear.

Toben winced. "Yeah, bum ride, Cody." He glanced at Poppy, who was watching him. How he wished he could tell what she was thinking.

He shook his head, smiling.

The boys tried to convince them to let them join the calf scramble even though the announcer said ten and up.

"Rowdy Barron White," Poppy chastised him. "Mitchell knows how old you are. Don't think he won't call you out on it."

Rowdy sighed.

"Rowdy Barron?" Toben asked, leaning closer. Damn but Poppy smelled sweet.

Poppy's eyes widened, her gaze falling to his lips. "After my dad…"

"Fitting," he agreed. "But he's a Boone."

Poppy frowned, her gaze darting to Rowdy, then back to him. "He wasn't a Boone until recently."

Toben couldn't argue that fact. "He is now."

"Ma," Rowdy interrupted. "Can we get some popcorn?"

He took the boys to get popcorn and bottled water, wandered through the stalls and ended up by the pens, looking at the broncs and bulls.

"He looks mean." Cody pointed at a massive bull with long horns.

Toben nodded.

"Ever want to ride again?" Rowdy asked.

Toben looked at his son and shook his head. "Nope. My rodeo days are behind me."

"That's okay, Dad—you did great," Rowdy said, taking his hand.

Toben squeezed his hand, smiling.

They made their way back to the stands to find Poppy and Tandy had admirers. "Dad." Rowdy sighed, shaking his head.

"And they took our seats," Cody added.

Toben climbed the bleachers, leading the boys up. He didn't have to say a thing. He didn't know if it was the look on his face or Rowdy's "Excuse me, you're sitting by my ma" that sent the men packing. Either way, they got their spots back.

Tandy and Cody headed out after the rodeo. Tandy offered to take Rowdy for a sleepover, but he wanted to stay and see the fireworks. Toben didn't argue. This was their first holiday together. They made their way to the concrete dance floor and found Renata on the stage, helping set up for the live music they'd brought in.

"Having a good time?" she asked.

"Yes, ma'am," Rowdy answered.

"He won the Mutton Bustin' tonight," Toben added. "Figure we should celebrate."

"I'll come find you once I'm done." Renata smiled. "Congratulations, Rowdy."

"Fireworks on the hill?" he asked.

She nodded.

"That's where we'll be, then." He took Rowdy's hand, stooping to listen to him ask a million questions. When he glanced back at Poppy, he couldn't help but notice the attention she was getting. Not that he could blame a man for looking. In her sequins, she drew the eye. Once they got a look at her, it was hard to look away. He and Rowdy stopped.

"What?" she asked.

"Thought we'd wait for you," Toben said.

"Yeah, Ma." Rowdy held out his other hand. "Dad said the best seats are up here."

The music started a few minutes later. Renata joined them, a thick blanket in hand. She spread it out and sat. "Now tell me all about your competition," she said to Rowdy.

Toben stood with Poppy, her agitation putting him on edge. He didn't know how to make this better.

By the time Rowdy had finished his story, the music had slowed and the faint popping of firecrackers had grabbed Rowdy's attention.

"Fireworks?" he asked, jumping up.

Renata pointed. "Look right over there, Rowdy. Should start any minute."

Poppy sighed, swaying slightly to the music. He didn't need any more encouragement than that. "Dance with me?" he asked.

She stiffened.

"It's just a dance," he murmured.

She stepped into his arms, rigid and stiff. Her eyes locked with his and took his breath away. He didn't know how to win her love, but as fireworks lit up the sky, he couldn't stop himself from whispering, "I love you, Poppy."

Chapter Seventeen

Poppy glanced at the clock. It was eight o'clock and she'd just rung up the last customer. She locked the door and turned over the sign to Closed. As far as openings went, she knew this one had been good. But she was tired and hoping one or two of the applications she'd received would be good enough to hire. Her dream had been to have her own shop, but that didn't mean she wanted to spend every hour of every day here.

She'd rather be with Rowdy and Toben. They'd had big plans for the day. She didn't know what their big mystery trip was about, but she knew they were picking up everything they'd need for Cheyenne before picking up the dog and taking her home.

It was so late and she was so tired she decided to see if she should bring something home for dinner. She called, but it went straight to voice mail.

She put the money in the safe, yawning, then flipped off the rest of the lights.

She heard sirens again, but there had been a lot of them these past couple of days. First the parade, then several small fires caused by people setting off fireworks. The grass was so dry it didn't take much to get a real blaze going.

As she stepped out and locked the front door, a fire truck

flew by, followed by an ambulance. She frowned, hoping everyone was okay.

She called Toben's phone again. Still no answer. Whatever they were doing, she hoped they were having fun. The prospect of Cheyenne's homecoming and a day alone with his father had Rowdy too excited to sleep even after the rodeo and fireworks the night before. She'd put him to bed, lying at his side until his breathing had steadied and the house had fallen quiet.

Only then did she go to bed, alone, missing the feel of Toben's heartbeat beneath her cheek. He'd told her he loved her, then helped her load Rowdy up—no expectation of anything else. She'd called Mitchell then, waking him up to spill her every fear and worry and hope and dream.

"Will you regret not giving him a chance, Poppy? You don't want to live with regret, trust me." Mitchell's mumbled answer had made her toss and turn the rest of the night.

She climbed into the truck and headed to the café, where she picked up a few burgers and milk shakes. Then she topped off her gas tank and headed home. She'd crossed the first bridge when a truck pulled up behind her, flashing its lights. She pulled onto the shoulder to let the truck pass. It didn't. It kept flashing until she stopped her truck. Her stomach twisted sharply, unease pricking up the hairs on the back of her neck.

Did Stonewall Crossing have undercover cops? But she hadn't been speeding. She looked in her rearview mirror…

"Poppy?" It was Fisher Boone. And Ryder. "You heading home?"

She nodded, rolling down the window. "Everything okay?"

Fisher and Ryder exchanged looks. "I need to tell you something, but I need you to stay calm. I'll drive, okay?" Fisher offered.

Ryder headed back to his truck, climbed in and flew past them.

"I can drive," she said, her throat tightening. "So tell me... What's going on?"

"There's a fire, Poppy. At your place." He opened her truck door. "Rowdy is fine."

A fire. Her mind went blank. A fire. She stared at Fisher. "A fire? Rowdy?" she repeated.

"He's fine. Rowdy is fine."

He was fine. Rowdy was fine. Her heart tightened, her chest so heavy it hurt to draw in breath. "Toben?" He had to be okay. Why was she was shaking, so hard and so fast her teeth were rattling? She repeated, panicking, "Toben?"

"He's okay. Let me drive."

"O-okay," she said, sliding over. "Fast."

The rest of the drive was a blur. She felt sick, her head and stomach unable to calm down, no matter how many times Fisher told her Rowdy was okay. She didn't believe it, couldn't. She had to see him, to hold him in her arms and breathe him in.

And Toben? He had to be all right—for both of them. She loved him. She needed him.

The sun was fading, but the column of black smoke was visible from the road. So much smoke. She tried not to imagine how scared Rowdy was. Toben was there. He'd keep him safe. She rubbed her hands on her thighs, shaking her head. The house didn't matter. As long as they were okay, that was all that mattered. *But, please, God, let them be okay.*

She was out of the truck before they'd come to a complete stop, staring at the smoking, blackened mess that had been her house...

She spun, the blood roaring in her ears. "Rowdy?" she called out, swallowing smoke and coughing. "Rowdy?" She forced the name out. She didn't see him. Her eyes burned, the heat and smoke reaching her. Where was he? "Rowdy!"

"Ma!" He came barreling across the yard, Cheyenne glued to his side.

She burst into tears, falling to her knees as she caught Rowdy close. She held him, burying her face in his hair. She hugged him tightly and ran her hands over his face. "Hi, baby," she whispered, her voice broken. "You okay?"

"Don't cry, Ma." Rowdy smiled. "Don't cry."

"He's okay." Toben's voice, so full of grief. "He's okay, Poppy."

"Dad took us to the barn, Ma. We were okay. He kept us safe." Rowdy stroked her hair.

She stared up at Toben, unable to stop the tears from flowing. She reached out, grabbed Toben's hand and yanked him down beside her. "Thank you." She wrapped them both in her arms. "You're safe. Both of you." She sucked in a deep breath. They were her whole world, right here. "You're safe."

Cheyenne wedged herself between them, making Rowdy laugh. "You should have seen her, Ma. She barked and barked and told us what was happening."

Poppy sat back on her knees, frantically wiping at her tears. "She did?"

"We were in the barn," Toben explained. "If she hadn't barked... Well, it happened pretty damn quick."

She stared at the house then. The kitchen was a black gaping hole, smoke billowing up and into the sky. The hoses kept going, soaking the ground around the house and saturating the roof.

"Ma?" Rowdy held her hand.

She looked at him, doing her best to smile.

"You okay?" he asked.

She laughed, sounding a little unhinged. She glanced at Toben, pleading for help. "I'm fine. It's silly, I know. I'm trying to stop." But it was hard. The fear had eased, but her relief was all-consuming.

"She was worried over you, Rowdy. It's what moms do." His hand stroked along her cheek. She leaned into his touch, letting him pull her into his arms. "It's okay, Poppy. I promise, it's going to be okay."

"It is," she whispered. "I know it. You're both okay."

"Right," Rowdy agreed. "We've got each other. And Cheyenne and Cheeto and Stormy. We're good."

Toben's arms tightened around her. "He's right."

She nodded, turning into his chest. "It's just…for a minute…" She shook her head, sitting back. "I didn't see him…" She blew out a wavering breath.

He nodded. "I'd never let anything happen to him." He stood, pulling her up with him.

"I know. But it was…you, too, Toben." She swallowed.

A crease formed between his brows. "You don't need to worry about me."

She stared at him dumbly. Of course she'd worried about him. She shook her head. He didn't know how she felt. She'd done too good a job of keeping it from him. And herself. "Toben—"

"Ma." Rowdy's hand grabbed hers. "Where are we going to sleep now?"

She stared at the smoking house, her son's question gutting her. Was it a total loss? The kitchen was gone and the rest wasn't livable—that much was clear. "A hotel?" She grinned at him, wanting to reassure him. "The apartment." The couch was small but comfy—it would work for Rowdy. And since she had no plans to let him out of her sight, she'd sleep on the floor next to him.

"The Lodge?" Toben asked, glancing at Fisher.

Fisher nodded. "Already on it. Dad's happy to put you up." He held out his cell phone. "You're family, after all."

"You're not alone," Toben whispered, his voice gruff. "You hear me?"

She felt tears welling in her eyes again, staring at the man she loved. "Yes, thank you."

"Can I bring Cheyenne?" Rowdy asked Fisher.

"Of course," Toben agreed. "I can bring Cheeto and Stormy over, too, if you want." His gaze shifted to her.

Poppy understood. The ground was dry. All the small fires. The firefighters were soaking the ground now, but there was no guarantee. She glanced at the barn, then Toben. No reason to risk it. "Please," she said, nodding. "If there's room?"

His crooked grin wrapped around her heart. "I'll make room." He nodded at Fisher. "Can you take them to the Lodge? I'll finish up here."

"You got it," Fisher said. "How about we get Cheyenne in the truck, Rowdy."

Poppy stared after Toben, hesitating before following him. "Toben."

He turned, the anguish on his face tearing at her insides. "Poppy," he groaned. He stared at the house, then her—his eyes red rimmed. "I'm so sorry. I'm so damn sorry."

She slid her arms around him, cradling his head against her shoulder. "You didn't do this. You're both fine. That's all that matters."

His arms tightened around her. He pressed a kiss to her forehead and released her. "I'll catch up to you."

She nodded, then hurried back to Rowdy. She sat in the backseat, holding her son tight and rubbing Cheyenne's soft black coat.

"She's a good dog, Ma," Rowdy said, yawning.

"She's the best dog ever, Rowdy." She kissed the top of his head.

TOBEN YAWNED, RUNNING a hand along the back of his neck. It was late, too late to wake Poppy or Rowdy. But if he didn't see his boy, he'd never get any sleep. Rowdy had never been in any danger, not really. Cheyenne had had a hold of Rowdy's pants and wouldn't let go. Toben had told him to stay put in the barn and then Toben had run, knowing Poppy's and Rowdy's lives were in the house. If he could salvage anything, he was damn well going to try. But the closer he got, the more he knew there was nothing he could do. The flames were roaring, sending off waves of heat—a warning he wasn't about to ignore. Better to stay with Rowdy than upset the boy further.

He'd called the fire department and stayed with his son, feeling useless and—worse—responsible.

"Room one," his uncle Teddy said, holding out the key. "You need some sleep, boy."

"What are you doing up?" Toben asked, taking the key.

"Wanted to see you safe and sound for myself before I turned in." His uncle came around the counter and hugged Toben. "I'm guessing that's how you're feeling right about now. You go check on your family and get some shut-eye."

"Yes, sir." Toben headed down the hall, stared at the door, then opened it.

Poppy lay in the far bed, almost hanging off the edge, to be near Rowdy. She'd want to stay close but not let Rowdy know how upset she was. And she had every reason to be upset. His heart was heavy with what might have been.

He sighed, looking at the second bed.

Cheyenne lay along Rowdy's side, sprawled across the bed. She lifted her head, saw him, yawned and lay back down. Toben closed the door and rubbed the dog's head. Apparently, she didn't see him as a threat.

He bent over Rowdy, smoothing his still-damp curls from his forehead and breathing in his son's sweet scent. All the panic of the day, of what could have happened, pressed in on him. "I love you," he murmured. "You're my boy." He kissed Rowdy's forehead once, then again, before resting his forehead against Rowdy's. It helped ease the ache somewhat.

Poppy's fingers gripped his jeans, tugging. He reached back, letting their fingers thread together. That was better, to have them both in his hold. He squeezed her hand. She squeezed right back. He drew in a slow breath, tucked the blanket over Rowdy and sat on the side of Poppy's bed. "I didn't mean to wake you."

"I'm glad you did."

"I just needed to see him." He looked at her, tracing her cheek. "And you."

She sat up, climbing into his lap.

"I haven't showered," he whispered, almost groaning at the feel of her soft and warm against him. She needed comfort right now, and so did he. If he held her long enough, maybe his fear would finally go away? He was willing to try.

"I don't care," she said, resting her head on his shoulder.

He chuckled, burying his nose in her hair.

"I found you," she said, her hands twisting in his knit shirt. "And I'm not going to let you go, Toben. You hear me?" She looked up at him, her whispered words raw and broken. "I don't care if you get bored or restless—you are stuck with us."

He stared at her. "I am?" His voice hitched.

"Yes. You are. Because you love us." She sniffed, tears falling onto her cheeks. "You love me."

"I do." He wiped the tears from her cheeks, his pulse kicking up. "So much."

She smiled. "I'm ready to believe you."

He grinned. "Then I'll tell you again. I love you, Poppy White. And, every damn day, I'll do my best to earn your love."

"Every *damn* day." She nodded. "You promise?"

"I was ready to promise before things went to hell." He reached into his pocket. "We had a big proposal worked out. Rowdy's got a romantic streak. You should see the barn," he said, holding up the ring they'd bought early that morning. "It was tied to Stormy's halter. There are flowers all over the barn...all over. I stuck myself a dozen times." He held his finger out for inspection. "I knew you'd say no, but I didn't care. I'll keep asking until you say yes."

She smiled, kissing each cut. "Yellow roses?"

"Of course." He nodded, loving the way she looked at him. "Asking you to marry me now, like this, isn't enough. You deserve more." He'd wanted it to be big and special. Something she'd remember always.

She shook her head and held her hand out. "Ask me."

He chuckled. "Maybe I'll wait."

She frowned at him. "No more waiting, Toben. Ask me tonight," she said, and pressed her lips to his. "Marry me tomorrow." She kissed him again. "Love me now."

He kissed her, his lips sealing them together and easing the ache in his chest. "I do, Poppy. Only, I know you could do better," he murmured.

"I *want* you. I love you," she said. "Even though Fisher said you were fine, I couldn't believe it. I saw that smoke... All I could think was...no. I love him. I need him...you. And I was too scared to tell you how much...I care. I thought admitting I loved you would chase you away."

He shook his head, frowning.

"I know." She smiled. "Now. So I want you to know—I need you to know. I love you so much, Toben Boone. You and only you. Whatever else happens, I want us to be a family. I'll fight to protect it."

She had no idea the power her words had over him. Her love washed the rest of the day's pain away. He had her. He had Rowdy. He had everything. He slipped the ring on her finger.

"You didn't ask." She laughed softly.

"After that, I didn't think I had to." He kissed her again. He loved the feel of her fingers in his hair, the brush of her nose along his cheek. "Will you marry me, Poppy?"

"Yes." She wrapped her arms around him, holding him tightly.

"Thank you, Poppy. For giving us—me—a second chance. I won't let you down," he promised, pressing a kiss against her lips.

Epilogue

"You look like a princess, Ma." Rowdy stood in his little gray tuxedo and felt cowboy hat, looking every bit the dashing cowboy.

"Well, I'm proud to have you as my handsome escort," she said. "Ready to take some pictures?"

Rowdy nodded. "I guess."

Poppy laughed, knowing how fond Rowdy was of pictures. Something else he and his father agreed on—pictures were torture. She followed her son to the barn, careful not to trip on her long white skirt, smiling at the friends and family that gathered for her and Toben's special day.

But something was poking her left foot, and it hurt. She paused in the barn and lifted her skirts, bracing herself against the wall to tug off her boot. A Lego block fell onto the hay at their feet.

Rowdy grinned. "Sorry, Ma. I was looking for that piece."

She laughed, a sudden movement catching her attention. "I thought he was going to behave," she murmured. Toben had been put out by her belief they should spend one last night apart and downright grumpy when she insisted they not see each other until the ceremony. "Toben?" she called out.

He was on the move, trying to avoid getting caught.

But she wasn't going to let that happen. She smoothed her skirts in place, did a quick search for her lariat and hurried out the back door. The cameraman was fast at her heels.

She was quiet, spinning her rope and letting it fly before Toben figured something was up. He turned, caught, her aim true. He looked so damn handsome he took her breath away. She tugged the rope and handed it to Rowdy. "Hold this, Rowdy. I need to teach your dad a lesson."

Rowdy giggled.

Poppy gripped the rope, tugging her soon-to-be husband forward while walking toward him. His surprise was replaced with something more. His blue eyes swept over her, his jaw locked, and his eyes sparkled. He shook his head, grabbed the rope and tugged her toward him.

"You are beautiful," he murmured, leaning forward for a kiss. "And I am the luckiest son of a gun in the whole world."

She pressed a finger to his lips. "That might be, but you're not getting a kiss until we're married."

He frowned. "Poppy, that's not right, now. Seeing you like this." He shook his head, his possessiveness downright thrilling. "Just a little one?"

"It'll teach you a lesson," she argued, knowing full well once they started, neither one would want to stop.

"Lesson learned." He tipped her chin back. "Next time, I'll listen."

She sighed, unable to resist him.

"Ma!" Rowdy wedged himself between them. "No kissing until after the preacher says you can."

Poppy laughed. "You heard your son, Toben."

Toben stared at her, then his son, defeated. "That preacher better talk fast."

"Come on, Ma." Rowdy took her hand, taking Toben's

with his other hand. "I know she's pretty, Dad, and you can kiss her all you want after—"

"She's my wife," Toben finished. "Let's get this wedding started."

Poppy saw his wink and shook her head.

"I love you, Poppy," he said, so sincere her breath hitched.

"I love you, too," she said.

"You still can't kiss," Rowdy said, tugging them toward the altar and the waiting preacher. "Not yet."

"After the wedding," Toben whispered as he leaned close, "prepare to be kissed."

* * * * *

If you loved this novel, don't miss the other books by Sasha Summers in her BOONES OF TEXAS *series:*

A COWBOY'S CHRISTMAS REUNION
TWINS FOR THE REBEL COWBOY
COURTED BY THE COWBOY
A COWBOY TO CALL DADDY

Available now from Harlequin Western Romance!

#1653 TEXAS REBELS: PAXTON

Texas Rebels • by Linda Warren

Paxton Rebel was the brother destined to never settle
down. When he falls hard for Remi Roberts, he gets more
than he bargained for...because she's in the middle of
adopting a child.

#1654 COWBOY DOCTOR

Sapphire Mountain Cowboys • by Rebecca Winters

The first call Roce Clayton receives after setting up his
veterinarian business on his family's ranch is quite serious.
A horse's life is in jeopardy...and so is the life of a beautiful
stranger, Tracey Marcroft.

#1655 HER COWBOY BOSS

Hope, Montana • by Patricia Johns

Working at the Harmon Ranch to meet the owner—her
biological father—is the craziest idea Avery Southerly has
ever had. Even worse: falling for her boss, ranch manager
Hank Granger!

#1656 THE RANCHER'S MIRACLE BABY

Men of Raintree Ranch • by April Arrington

When rancher Alex Weston takes in Tammy Jenkins and
an orphaned baby during a storm, his quiet life is turned
upside down. Falling for his temporary family was never
part of the plan!

HWESTCNM0717

"What are you doing letting a Rebel into your house?" Remi
turned on her grandmother.

Miss Bertie shrugged. "I have nothing against the
Rebels."

"John Rebel killed my father. Have you forgotten that?"

Oh, *crap.* It dawned on Paxton for the first time. This had
to be Ezra McCray's daughter.

"Okay, missy, I'm not standing here and letting you paint
your father as a saint. Everyone in this town was scared of
him. And in case you've forgotten, he tried to kill two of the
Rebel boys."

"I'd rather not talk about this, and I'd rather not talk to
him." She nodded toward Paxton.

"Do you know what he's doing here?" Miss Bertie asked.

"No."

"He helped me haul my calves to the auction barn today."

"Gran—"

Paxton had had enough. He wasn't stepping into this land
mine. He handed Miss Bertie the papers. "You can pick up
your check tomorrow afternoon." He tipped his hat. "It's
been a pleasure."

"Wait a minute. I want to look at this," Miss Bertie called, and he forced himself to stop and turn around. "I have to find my glasses." She disappeared down a hallway.

Remi stepped farther into the room. "What are you doing here?"

"Your grandmother just told you. I hauled her calves to the auction."

"There was no need."

"Oh, and who was going to do it? You?"

"I could have."

"I don't think so. You're not well." The moment the words left his mouth he knew they were not something you said to a woman. And he was right. Her sea-green eyes simmered with anger.

She moved closer to him. "I'm fine. Do you hear me? I'm fine." She wagged one long finger in his face. "I'm fine."

He did the only thing a red-blooded cowboy could do. He bit her finger.

She jumped back. "You bit me!"

"I'm going to keep biting you until you admit the truth."

"You…you…stay away from my grandmother." She turned and pranced into the living room.

"A thank-you would have been nice!" he shouted to her back.

He walked out and shoved the shift of his pickup into gear, backing up and leaving the crazy ladies behind. He was sticking his nose into something that didn't concern him. And he had no desire to get to know Ezra McCray's daughter.

*Don't miss TEXAS REBELS: PAXTON
by Linda Warren, available August 2017
wherever Harlequin® Western Romance
books and ebooks are sold.*

www.Harlequin.com

LOVE
Harlequin
romance?

Join our Harlequin community to share your thoughts and connect with other romance readers!

Be the first to find out about promotions, news, and exclusive content!

Sign up for the Harlequin e-newsletter and download a free book from any series at

www.TryHarlequin.com

CONNECT WITH US AT:

Harlequin.com/Community

Facebook.com/HarlequinBooks

Twitter.com/HarlequinBooks

Instagram.com/HarlequinBooks

Pinterest.com/HarlequinBooks

ReaderService.com

HARLEQUIN®

**ROMANCE WHEN
YOU NEED IT**

HSOCIAL2017

Looking for more satisfying love stories
with community and family at their core?

Check out **Harlequin**® Special Edition and **Harlequin**® Western Romance books!

New books available every month!